ANDREW'S PIANO

by

ART MYERS

2016

ISBN 978-1-7357208-1-4

Cover design by Janet L. Blankenship

Contact Art Myers: artmyersbooks@gmail.com

For Jeanne

Who has been there the whole time.

Other Books by Art Myers

MY STORY*
How A Young Boy From California
Ended Up An Old Man In Florida

A NEW LIFE FOR ROBERT JOHNSON

10,000 YEARS – Before Present*

ED ADAMS CHASES A DREAM

*Publication pending

ANDREW'S PIANO

PREFACE

This is a work of fiction. Andrew's piano never existed. Neither, therefore, did it's magical powers that made it possible for Andrew Miller to play it as he does in the story.

However the location, Loveland, Colorado, is real. Several of the characters are based on real people. Their names have been changed slightly but most of them, and their acquaintances, will easily recognize who they are. The places are also, for the most part, real although some by necessity are fictionalized.

Andy and his wife Jan are, with apologies from the author, based on the author and his wife. They lived in Loveland from 1986 to 2002. The story is placed in the first two years of this time frame. Professionally during the time of the the story he was a sculptor and she was a realtor, as they were during their entire time in Loveland. The author attended the IRS auction which did occur at a foundry, occupied the upstairs studio described for two years, and they rented the town home on Taft Avenue during the same time period. One evening they attended a party that had a Steinway Grand Piano in the host's living room. The six others of the group of eight friends in the story are fictional composites. Adelita's Restaurant is still in business, the Rialto Theater is open, and the Benson Park Sculpture Garden is one of the best, if not the best, sculpture garden in the United States.

The author does acknowledge the simplifying of the Piano's restoration descriptions as presented. Especially the fitting, stringing, tuning, regulation and voicing which require craftsmanship and experience far beyond that presented. Some was assumed to have been previously accomplished but to bring Andrew's piano to the level as in the story would have required much more.

You are asked to read "Andrew's Piano" just for enjoyment and if possible listen to some classical or jazz piano for background. In this story the Steinway Model C Parlor Grand Piano, about 1928 New York build, is the star. Those that compose and those that play the music for and on these beautiful pianos are the ones to thank.

Just maybe, it could have happened.

CHAPTER 1

Andy Miller had just climbed the stairs to his rented second floor studio on Jefferson Ave, between Third and Fourth Street, opened the door and looked around his space. He had several sculptures underway, the biggest a half scale Bald Eagle which was what he would work on today. It was a comfortable work space and in the same building were four other sculptors in similar sized studios, two on the first floor and three on the second. Each studio had space, good lighting, and a full bathroom. Even better they were located in the heart of Loveland, Colorado's sculptors community.

Andy and his wife Jan had moved to Loveland shortly after a two year engineering job in Illinois had come to an end and it had been decided it was time for him to get back into his previous career in sculpture. They had rented a comfortable town home on Taft Avenue, just a few miles to the west, and were just completing their first year here. Jan had started a new career in real estate sales and had managed to quickly join a very good group of realtors.

No sooner had Andy opened his door than Bill Holstead from the studio on the backside of the building showed up. "What are you doing this morning?" No good morning or how are you but that was normal as he and Andy had become good friends. Bill had arrived in Loveland a few months after Andy and Jan, was a bachelor and was living in his studio.

"Not much," was Andy's answer.

"The IRS auction of the Thomas Collins foundry is this morning and I am going up to see what's there. Want to go?" Bill asked handing Andy the flier with a partial list of auction items and the particulars. There wasn't much he really needed but it might be a fun way to spend the morning and he didn't have any time pressures at the moment.

"Sure. Looks like it could be interesting. I'll even drive."

The building would be open for previewing by the time they got there and the auction was to start promptly at 10:00 am. Thomas Collins was a very good sculptor and specialized in wildlife, especially birds. As his sales grew he opened his own foundry to cast his works and cast for a number of other local sculptors. The rumor was that his problems with the IRS had to do with the non-payment to them of the with-holdings from his employees pay checks or maybe it was just his not collecting them. Part of the settlement was the seizure of his foundry and its contents.

As Andy and Bill approached the foundry the number of cars and trucks surprised them both. "What do you think? Is it worth going in there? What are all these people doing here?" was Bill's immediate reaction.

"Might as well take a look since we're here. You never know what may be in there that you can't live without," was Andy's prophetic answer.

Entering the front office found it jammed with people but fortunately there was a clear path to the desk where you signed in and got your auction paddle. It was very efficient. Name and address, telephone number, drivers license for verification, and a blank check from your bank. Sign on the line and get your drivers license back with your auction paddle. Number 167 for Andy and 168 for Bill. All done in just a couple of minutes with instructions that the auction would start in ten minutes, would be fast, and all sales would be final and had to be paid for in full that day.

Andy looked around the office and could see nothing of interest. There was one of Collins's bird sculptures, a nice one, but other than that most of the office items looked to be of little value. Bill gave Andy a nod and, thinking the same thing, they exited the office and went out to the main foundry floor. There was a crowd there also. It was going to be a mad house but they were inside so started to make the tour. The large foundry equipment wasn't of interest. There was a small box of very used metal chasing tools on one of the work benches that might be worth a bid and in a storage area a number of walnut and marble bases of interest except they all had been drilled for Collins's pieces.

The call for the start of the auction was made and Andy and Bill got close enough to the office door to hear the instructions. Again it was emphasized that this would be a fast auction and if you wanted to win a bid, bid fast and often. They would start in the office and follow the numbers which were labeled on each item. Number one was called and off the auction went with bids being made at what seemed to both Andy and Bill to be way too high.

"What the hell are these guys thinking?" Bill said to Andy and to all those around them. "Holy cow!"

The crowd started pushing into the main foundry as the auction progressed and it was going fast. The biding still seemed to be on the high side. The small box of tools arrived in about forty-five minutes and were immediately bid at twice what Andy thought they were worth. You could almost buy new ones for what the final bid was called out.

The main foundry casting equipment was getting closer on the auction list and the crowd was now pushing about and creating a dust up. Andy and Bill got separated and Andy ended up behind a large boiler like piece of equipment that was used to heat up and melt out the wax replicas from the investment molds.

There was some space there and he welcomed the relief from crowd. The auction was indeed going fast and it was obvious a number of the bidders knew what they wanted and what they were willing to pay. Andy having no interest in any of the remainder of the auction items started looking about the small area he had literally been pushed into. Back in the corner, obscured by both shadow and a thick layer of dust, was the body of what looked like a big piano. Curious, Andy took a closer look and that's what it was but it was in pieces. It was leaning against the wall with the end where the key board should be on the floor. There were no strings. The legs and a frame with three pedals were placed inside the body as was a large wrapped piece, all covered in the thick coating of foundry dust. More big parts were behind the body and two medium sized card board boxes sealed by tape were stacked alongside.

Andy was suddenly interested. He decided to wipe some of the dust off the curved side of the piano body with his hand. He was startled by an odd sensation he felt and jerked his hand back. It was almost like touching a living thing when what you expected was just a dusty piece of wood. He then put his hand back in the same place and brushed away some more of the dust. As he did this he felt a more distinct sensation and it seemed the noise of the auction faded away and the meager light lessened. He again removed his hand and the noise and light returned to normal. He was now a little nervous and looked around to see if anyone was watching. He was alone in the corner and this time he placed his hand firmly on the piano and slid it along the contour. There was no doubt about the sensation as it passed from his hand up his arm and into his chest. The noise abated to almost silence, the light dimmed dramatically and the dust floating about had the gold of bronze particles sparkling in profusion.

Andy pulled his hand away slowly this time and the auction came back into focus. The auctioneer was now starting the bidding on big boiler in front of him and quickly item 287 was hammered sold. Before he thought about what he was doing Andy pushed forward and called out, "How about the piano parts over here? I can't find a number on them."

"What did you call them? Piano parts! We don't have any listing for piano parts." The auctioneer looked at his assistant and she said, "Nope!"

The Auctioneer yelled out, "Item 287A is added to the list. Piano parts. What am I bid for piano parts?" There was laughter in the crowd and he called out, "One hundred. Am I bid one hundred dollars."

Andy raised his paddle.

"Sold to 167 for one hundred dollars," the Auctioneer yelled out to a laughing and applauding crowd.

And then on they went to 288 while Andy went back to his piano.

CHAPTER 2

Andy stood in front of the piano. "What have I done?" he thought. The piano cabinet was huge. Over seven feet high as it leaned against the foundry wall and maybe five feet wide at it's base. There was a flat wooden interior panel mounted inside the cabinet with the three heavy looking legs and the frame holding three foot pedals leaned against it. The bundled piece was about five feet tall, maybe two feet wide and was wrapped in dirty black plastic. All were covered in years of foundry dust. Behind the cabinet was a top piece of two parts hinged together and behind that a big cast iron framework which looked somewhat harp shaped and appeared to be heavy. The two boxes were securely taped but the cardboard was aged and starting to come apart.

It was then he noticed for the first time that the cabinet, legs, and the top piece were painted a ghastly off white color with streaks of gold brush marks looking like the old antiquing furniture paint from the 1950's.

Bill came up behind Andy and blurted out, "What the hell did you just do? I heard sold to one-sixty-seven along with a bunch of laughter and applause. Man, look at that beast."

Andy felt a tinge of panic and thought maybe he

had really stepped into the proverbial stuff this time. His next thought was of Jan and how and what he could tell her of the why of what he had just done. Their budget was really tight and even a hundred dollars was big. He was in some kind trouble.

"Boy is Jan going to be happy seeing that thing in your garage. I was hoping to be invited to dinner at your place tonight but I'll wait a few days." Bill put his hand on Andy's shoulder. "You done did it this time my friend."

"Thanks for the support," muttered Andy and then, "Come over here and put your hand where I brushed off the dust. Just hold it there. Tell me what you feel."

Bill put his hand on the contour part of the cabinet where Andy had felt the strange sensations. He brushed some more dust off, pressed his hand down and then turned to Andy. "Just a dirty piece wood and that ugly paint. Man that is one ugly paint job. Why would anyone paint a piano like that?"

Andy then placed his hand on the same spot and for a moment nothing happened. Then it was there again, even stronger than before, and he had no doubt something very strange and special was happening. "You didn't feel anything unusual?"

"Nothing"

Reassured, Andy started thinking how they could move this monster. He wanted to get the smaller pieces and the boxes out before leaving and then could plan coming back in the morning to get the two big ones.

"I am going to the desk and see if we can take the smaller stuff with us today and pick up the rest tomorrow. Wait for me here and I'll be right back." Bill nodded his head but wasn't smiling.

8

Andrew's Piano

At the desk the lady took Andy's check and said they usually wanted everyone to come back the next day for pick up but if he could hand carry the things out he could start as soon as the auction was over. She thought about another half hour. Andy headed back to let Bill know what was happening and they started to place the legs, pedal assembly, the bundled piece and the two boxes along the wall trying to get as much of the dust brushed off as possible.

With a little time remaining they moved the big cabinet just enough to look behind it and thought they could also take the lid and a couple of other smaller pieces that were there. The harp shaped cast iron frame was really heavy and the cabinet was so big they would need to get a trailer to haul them in.

Andy moved his van close to the foundry's big bay doors and fortunately they were on the end of the building where the piano was located. When the auction ended the doors were opened and after showing his paid receipt they were able to load up the van with four quick trips. Arrangements were made to return first thing in the morning to pick up the remaining two big pieces.

As they drove back neither spoke for awhile then Bill asked, in a conciliatory way, "What are you going to tell her."

"I'm not sure. Got any suggestions? How about 'The devil made me do it.'?"

"Andy, I don't think that will work."

Andy backed the van up to the town home's garage and raised the garage door. It was just after two and fortunately Jan was still at work. They quickly unloaded the van and placed all the parts along the left side wall. It really didn't look that bad except for the paint job and Andy covered most of the parts with a tarp.

"You got few minutes? I'd like to unwrap this one," Andy asked, pointing out the five by two foot package.

"Fine by me. The days most gone, anyway."

Andy pulled the tape off the black plastic and then removed the plastic. There laid the keyboard and for the first time since he held up the auction paddle he felt that all was not lost. It was the keyboard assembly. The ivory and ebony keys were beautiful, clean and the whole contraption looked as if it had been totally restored. It had value. Andy knew immediately that it was certainly worth a lot more than a hundred dollars. He was sure of that.

Bill whistled. "Maybe I should plan on coming to dinner after all."

"I tell you what. How about tomorrow evening after you help get the rest of my fantastic purchase down here?"

Andrew's Piano

CHAPTER 3

Andy took Bill back to the studio and then crossed the street to George Patterson's place. George was one of the best sculptors in the country and not only had a big studio and gallery but a complete operation to produce his works with the exception of the metal casting. His building also housed a number of studios and he was a partner in the small studio complex Andy and Bill were in. He was very supportive of all the town's sculptors and allowed rental of a portion of his metal chasing and patina areas when space was available. Andy made use of this on numerous occasions as it was convenient and a much better environment than renting space at one of the foundries. George was one of the truly nice guys.

Walking into his office area, Andy found him there next to his gallery manager's desk. As usual he was greeted warmly with, "Hi Andy. How are things going?"

"Pretty good, at least until today. Bill and I went up to the auction at Collins's foundry and I managed to buy something I need a trailer to get it back to the house. Wondered if I could borrow yours tomorrow morning for a couple hours?"

"Yeah, I heard about that. Collins was, well is, a good sculptor and ran a good foundry but I guess he was-

11

n't a very good book keeper. The trailer, sure. You got the hook up don't you?"

"Yep. I will be over about eight-thirty and should have it back here by eleven, if that's okay," Andy responded with obvious appreciation.

George was of course a bit curious of what Andy could have bought at the foundry that would require a trailer so he asked, "What did you buy up there that is that big, for crying out loud?"

A bit sheepishly Andy answered, "A piano."

"A what?"

"A piano. George, it is a story that you will have to wait a bit for. I know it will get around soon enough but I am not ready to talk about it right now. Trust me, you will have a lot of fun at my expense when it all comes out. Eight-thirty okay?"

"Eight-thirty will be fine."

Andy headed back to the town home with his head spinning as to what he fore saw as the gossip train going into full speed on his buying a piano at a foundry auction. It was just too good not to spread like wildfire and he was sure George had already told at least two people.

He parked outside the garage on the left side and raced in to take a closer look at the keyboard. It looked just as good as when he saw it thirty minutes ago. Andy found a big towel and covered the dinning room table and brought it in from the garage. He thought, "Man is this pretty."

Putting a finger on one of the keys he pressed down and one of the hammers jumped up. Then pressed another key, and another, and another. He remembered way back when he was about ten or twelve years old taking piano lessons, at his mother's insistence, and how awkward he felt. How he didn't want to play a piano. He wanted to be outside riding his bike or shooting hoops in the back yard. The piano lessons lasted about three months when the teacher told his mother there was no hope and she relented.

But now something was different. He rearranged his position and spread his fingers some and started to press several keys at the same time and moving about the keyboard mimicking pianists he had seen on television. The hammers bounced up and down, the movement seeming almost magical. Andy felt comfortable doing this, in a strange way, even knowing he was just playing around as a child might. Since there was no sound his foolishness had no feed back. He could pretend he was a pianist. For some reason it felt good.

The sound of the garage door opening drifted in breaking the spell. Jan came in through the garage entry and called out, "I'm home. How come you parked outside?" She dropped her purse and briefcase on the dryer and rounded the corner from the kitchen and stopped. "What is that?" was almost a shout. "What is that?" she repeated.

"It is a piano keyboard thing," was the best Andy could do.

"And just where did that come from and what is it doing on the dining room table?"

Andy was trapped. He started to speak, then paused, tried again and failed. This was not going well, he thought.

"Andy Miller, what have you done?" This time it was with a little more force and there was no smile on

Jan's pretty face, more like a dark cloud.

"Let me explain. At least try to."

Andy took a deep breath and started with describing the trip to the IRS auction with Bill. Once he got to the part about being pushed into the corner by the crowd and first seeing the piano Jan broke in, speaking very slowly and clearly.

"You mean you bought a whole piano? You don't know how to play a piano. We don't have room for a piano." She paused then continued, "Oh my God, how much did you spend?"

"Just a hundred dollars," Andy answered trying to make it sound like a trivial amount, which didn't work.

Jan came around the table, sat down opposite Andy, and looked directly at him over the keyboard. Andy pressed a key and a hammer jumped up. He then pressed another and it's hammer jumped, then several more in rapid succession. Jane just stared and then started to laugh.

Andy let a small smile start on his face and said "The devil made me do it."

CHAPTER 4

Last night had turned out alright. After Jan had a good laugh, and Andy thought she had seen value in the keyboard, he didn't think the money was a problem. Since she hadn't paid any attention to the parts in the garage he had a little more time to think about what to tell her next. His reaction on touching the piano cabinet would have to wait until later, maybe much later. Telling her his thinking about restoring the piano himself was also going to be delayed.

Following dinner, which was good as it always was, they had watched a little television and retired for the evening at nine as was becoming their habit. Andy couldn't sleep. His thoughts were running at high speed. First he had to learn all he could about restoration, the vocabulary of the piano, potential costs and potential pit-falls. Even more worrisome was how Jan could be convinced it would be worth it. He had two other big interruptions in his sculpture career since its start shortly after he was laid off as an engineer working in "the military industrial complex" fifteen years ago. They were just now getting started again, the third try.

After about an hour Andy got out of bed, donned a sweater over his pajamas and headed for the garage. Barefoot, he went over to the boxes and pulled off the tape on the first box. The side of the box came apart and a slew of smaller boxes fell on the floor. They were imprinted "Genuine Steinway Parts" and were of several different sizes. Andy opened the first one he picked up and it was packed with packets containing what could only be piano strings. "Oh boy!" thought Andy. His hundred dollar investment was looking better and better.

After he had stacked up the ones from the first box, it was on to the second box. Again the sides fell apart when the tape was cut and this time variety of bagged, boxed, and loose items presented themselves on the floor. This time they were obviously parts, hundreds of them, from the piano and it would take some time to sort and identify them all. The three big brass casters were recognizable and looked to be in pretty good shape. Andy knew he could clean and polish these up to look great and function perfectly. He found a couple of boxes he had on hand and packed away all the loose items leaving the casters out for show. It could be all of the parts needed for the restoration were here.

Someone had started the restoration, then packed it all up and stashed it in the corner of Thomas Collins's foundry. He would have to do a little searching to find out who. Collins was reported to still be in Colorado but no one seemed to know exactly where. There even was a rumor he was in jail. Andy knew he would have to at least try to get the full story on the piano's history before he got too involved with the restoration. The sensation he had felt on those first touches of the cabinet were so real that he felt certain that he must bring the piano back to life. He even felt the keyboard was sending him a message.

Andy slipped back into bed and it was a bit after two before he finally fell asleep.

He was at George's at eight-thirty sharp and Bill was waiting for him. They hooked up the trailer and headed up to the foundry building. He had put a furniture dolly, several packing blankets, rope and straps in the van. When they arrived the big bay doors were open and Andy found a space so that they could reach the van with the dolly on the concrete driveway. Several large trucks were there as the big equipment would have to be prepped for moving and other things moved about in order to get the lifting equipment in place.

Andy and Bill quickly got the big cabinet's flat side on the dolly and in no time had it in the trailer, padded and lashed down. It was back for the big cast iron harp and it proved more of a challenge as it's weight and height made it unstable on the dolly. A couple of the other workers offered help and soon it too was secured in the trailer. All said it took only twenty minutes to load up.

"Piece of cake" Andy exclaimed.

Bill responding "Now all we have to do is unload it without damaging us. Or more importantly me."

Part way back Bill couldn't wait any longer. "What did Jan say?"

"Bill, we had a good laugh. She fixed me a good dinner and actually seemed to think it was okay. Even gave me a little back rub before she fell asleep. I am a lucky guy."

"Wait til she sees these two. Especially that beautiful white antiqued cabinet."

Andy's little dark cloud showed up and he knew this would be a test and when he got to the restoration idea it would be a major one. He did have the keyboard assembly and the boxes of strings and other parts. They have value. He could always just sell them if he had to.

CHAPTER 5

The big cabinet and the harp were off loaded and leaned against the garage wall. Lots of adjusting got everything spaced such that each part was available without having to move any of the others about. The tarp covered all the smaller pieces and the harp but unfortunately the "beast" was too big to hide. The paint really looked awful and it dominated the scene. There was no way Jan would not see it, and it alone, when she first drove into the garage.

"I could try to cover it up with some plastic," Andy moaned.

"No way to hide that thing Andy. Take me back to my studio. Let me know tomorrow how it goes at your house tonight. You can always sleep in your studio if you have to," Bill chortled.

Andy dropped Bill off and returned George's trailer. It was just before eleven so he went up to his studio and started working on the eagle sculpture. He was working in wax and having done most of the modeling work was now starting the detailing, shaping the feathers and lining in the shafts and barbs. It was slow work and required concentration. The piano keep coming into his thoughts and by two o'clock he couldn't do one more feather, so he headed home.

The big cabinet was in the same position as it was in the foundry but the garage lights were much brighter and the awful paint looked even worse. Andy was almost afraid to put his hand on the area where the sensation he experienced at the foundry was felt as what if it wasn't there anymore. He could always sell the parts or the whole lot together. But he now wanted to restore it and hear what it would sound like. He was even thinking he might try to learn to play it despite his obvious history of no musical talent. He thought, "I must be nuts."

Andy walked over to the cabinet and very slowly placed his hand on the contour in an almost tender caress, then pressed firmly down. On it came. The sensation was stronger than ever running from his finger tips, up his arm and into his chest. The feeling of a comfort, confidence, and even desire was almost overwhelming. Again the lights seemed to dim and sounds were muted. There was no doubt that this was real and that he was to bring this piano back to life. To make it beautiful and play like the finest instrument of its kind. He was under some kind of spell and felt he had no other choice.

A bit shaken Andy removed his hand and said, "You win, I will take care of you." He then realized he was talking to a piano and thought that maybe he was going a bit crazy. But so what, this was something miraculous and he had to find out what it all meant.

He got his tape rule and measured the piano. From the top of the cabinet as it leaned against the wall to the bottom board where the keyboard assembly mounted was seven feet five inches and the width at the widest point was five feet one inch. He went into the house to his computer and going on line searched for Grand Piano dimensions. Up popped a link to Steinway Grand Piano dimensions and there was one on the list with the exact ones he had just measured. The Model C Parlor Concert Grand. If his piano was a Steinway that would be great news. He searched for identifying a Steinway Grand Piano Model C and a photo of the locations where the name and serial number were located was shown to be on the harp, with the them pin-pointed.

He raced back into the garage and uncovered the harp. Where the raised part of the casting having the signature should be only the raised area was evident and looked like what ever had been there had been ground off. Likewise, the serial number was missing. Everything else, even several details, looked exactly like those in the photograph. It could very well be a Steinway and that made Andy think that he may have made a really big score.

Andy was standing there thinking it was now time to do some real homework when the garage door started to go up. He had lost track of time and Jan would very shortly come into view as the door raised and he was standing next to one big piece of an ugly piano looking like a deer caught in the headlights.

She pulled in and Andy could see her eyes were not on him but on the "beast". Jan just sat in her car and stared at the piano cabinet and that dark look she would get when annoyed covered her face. She finally opened the car door, grabbed her purse and brief case and headed into the house. She did not speak or acknowledge Andy's presence. He waited a few moments then followed her in and firmly but politely spoke.

"Jan I want you to let me say something to you and

I want you to listen. There is a very good chance this is a Steinway Model C, the Parlor Concert Grand, and if it is it's worth a lot of money, even in the condition as you see it now. Refurbished it will be worth a lot more, and if it is in the right span of years, even more. She stood still just staring at him, then lowered her head and quietly said, "Okay," then turned away heading to the bedroom, entering and closing the door behind her.

Andy thought again, "You could sell the parts," and then, "No I can't!"

CHAPTER 6

Dinner that night was very quiet. Jan did ask a few more questions about the piano but none required much of a response from Andy. She then told him what her fears were and they were understandable.

"Andy, this is the third time you have essentially started over again in sculpture. The start was sort of a fluke after your layoff when we were in California and then the move to Aspen, which was a great time, but you changed from metal sculpture to bronze. When it was clear we couldn't afford to stay there any longer, the two years in Illinois with the PC engineering job was good for us financially until it came to an end and now we are starting over here in Loveland. You are just starting to do some really good work and your first pieces are starting to sell. What I am fearing is this piano may be another distraction and that it will halt your progress. I am making some money now but will it be enough? I'm scared, Andy. Really frightened."

There was nothing he could really say to Jan as she was right. He decided he would try to find the words to comfort her and also be truthful but wouldn't mention the contact he seemed to be making with the inanimate piano.

"Here's what I would like to do, at least for now. I

will keep working on my sculpture the majority of my time. I hope to finish the big eagle in the next few days and then it will take about a week to make the molds, pour and chase the waxes, and get them to the foundry. Their schedule is running about two weeks and during that time I can get close to finishing the other two small works. The only time I will spend on the piano will be to do research and maybe sort through all the parts. If it turns out it is a Steinway, and worth what I think it might be, we will then decide how to proceed."

Jan seemed to be okay with this and just said, "I can live with that. So far things have always worked out okay for us. You always amaze me with what you are able to do but this time I feel something is very different. That I am about to lose you."

"There is no chance of that," was Andy's quick response.

Morning was a bit more positive and Andy and Jan were off to work in an almost normal way. For Andy sometimes things work out that you don't expect and when he went down to the music store on Fourth Street, just three blocks from his studio, one of those things happened. He had spent three hours straight that morning doing feathers and was starting to cramp up. Two days of concentration and he had only the bottom sides of the wing's feathers left to do. Taking a break he walked up Fourth Street and entered the store.

The owner was behind the counter and the store had mostly school type instruments and a large number of guitars, drum sets, amplifiers and speakers.

"Hi, I'm Andy Miller, one of the sculptors in town. I bought a piano at an auction a week ago and I am trying to find out what kind and make it is. I don't want you to think I am naive but I think it may be a Steinway. It's measurements match the Model C exactly but where the ID should be it has been ground off. Would you know about pianos. And by the way it's all in parts."

"Jim Johnston, Andy, glad to meet you. I don't know much about pianos and even less about Steinways. I do know a gentleman in Loveland that not only knows all about them but has a collector's Steinway in his house and loves playing it for friends and quests. He would jump at the chance to look at yours."

Jim took out his address book, thumbed the pages and then wrote down the particulars on the back of one of his business cards. "Jason Roberts, here is his phone number. I'd call him after seven in the evening and definitely not before noon. I guarantee that when you mention Steinway he will want to see what you have."

Andy thanked Jim and headed back to his studio. He was excited. He had done some internet searches and, as always, seemed surprised that he had been able to get so much information. He downloaded a page titled Grand Piano Cabinet and it had a diagram with all the visible parts identified. Andy could now at least describe the parts he had by their real names. Another one showed the inside components. The Harp could also be called the Frame, the keyboard assembly was the Action or Keyboard and Action. It looked like when together just Action was the acceptable terminology. It was a start but he would get there.

Jan came home that evening with a big smile and handed Andy an envelop from her office. "Open it." Andy did. It was a nice big closing check. A hug, kiss and his usual "What a Woman!" helped out. She asked about his day and Andy told her he would be starting the mold making for the eagle sculpture tomorrow afternoon.

After dinner he described his trip to the music store and getting the name of a man here in Loveland that knows all about Steinway pianos. Jan seemed okay with that so Andy asked her if he should call right away, like tonight. She quickly answered, "Sure, the sooner we find out what that collection of stuff is in the garage the sooner we will know what to do with it." This had surprised Andy but he got the phone and called Jason Roberts.

He answered on the second ring and Andy introduced himself and told him how he got his number. Jason told Andy that Jim had called him that afternoon about giving his number out to this guy who thought he had a Steinway in parts. "When can I come over to see what you've got? How about right now?"

Jane could hear the conversation as Jason talked loud. Andy was looking at her she nodded yes. Andy responded, "Sure. We live at eleven hundred Taft, Unit thirty-nine."

Jason cut in, "I know right where that is. I am ten minutes away. Right now okay?"

"Come on over. I would really like to know what I have in the garage."

Ten minutes later there was a knock on the door and Jason Roberts entered not only their home but also their lives. Jason was several inches shorter than Andy's six feet. A little older, maybe mid sixties, just a bit over weight, with a round face that sported an infectious smile. A quick, "Hi," was followed by, "Where is it?"

Andy smiled at Jan and took Jason into the garage. He had taken the coverings off and the Action was on a small rolling work bench. Jason's first view was responded with "My God in heaven what have they done to this." He rushed over and started looking and touching each piece quickly and then was on to the next one. Andy could see he was excited. He stopped at the Action, pressed a few keys and smiled. "This has been restored and looks perfect. Your lucky with that. The Case looks right if you can ignore the paint, the Soundboard looks good and now let me look at the Frame."

Jason ran his hand over it, looking intently at the raised part of the casting that Andy had checked for the identifying signature. Jason took a pencil flashlight out of his pocket and shined it on that area at several different angles, rubbing a finger over the ground off area. He looked up and said to Andy "This is a Steinway Model C. No doubt about it. And even better is that I am pretty sure it is a 1920 to 1936 build. You have something very, very special here. Wow!"

CHAPTER 7

The three of them stood among the parts and the giant cabinet, with it's awful paint, looming over them. Andy looked shocked, Jason so excited he could barely contain himself, and Jan with an expression of fright. Jason turned to Andy and asked "Can we take the Action inside where there's better light so I can take a careful look?"

"Sure." Andy lifted it off the work bench and headed through the door. "Jan can you put the blanket on the table for me? Jan?"

Jan had hesitated as if she hadn't heard Andy but then jumped ahead of them and got the blanket spread. Andy set the Action back in the place where she had seen it first. They arranged the chairs giving Jason the one in front and he was immediately examining every detail. Jan offered coffee and Jason nodded yes. She went in the kitchen and returned with two cups as Andy would only take a sip from hers if he had any at all.

"It is in great condition. Completely refurbished and ready to use. Isn't it just beautiful?" Jason's face radiated his excitement. He then started to press the keys, running up and down the scale, fingering cords and rapidly repeating pressing of single keys. The hammers danced.

"Marvelous. I can't wait until it is back where it belongs and we can hear the sounds and tone of this great piano. Andy, you are going to do it aren't you? Restore it?"

Andy could feel Jan's stare and he was afraid to look at her. He choose his words carefully. "Jason, I'm trying to think this thing out. I am in a pretty important place in my sculpture career right now. You don't need to know the whole story, but let us just say for now the timing is not too good. Jan is just starting to make strides in real estate but we are not in shape financially to take on a big risk. We are going to think about it. I want to do it and I think I could."

Andy wasn't sure that this had come out as intended and Jason picked up the message that maybe Jan was not too enthused at the prospect. He jumped at the chance to add some fuel to the thought of the restoration. "Let me give you a little history about the Model C. Is that okay with you both?"

Andy looked at Jan, she nodded yes and actually smiled. Maybe this would work out after all. "Yes. I would like that," Andy answered for both of them.

"The first Model C was manufactured in 1878 by Steinway and Sons and was seven feet two inches, seven octave, 85-note piano. It was based on the earlier Parlor Grands being built by Steinway at the time. By 1880 the curved Case, you called it the cabinet, design was incorporated and was built until 1886. The Model C was then extensively redesigned with a 88-note keyboard and now was seven feet five inches. In 1896 they reshaped the case calling it the "New Curve" Model C. Production ceased in 1936 in New York but was continued in Hamburg and are still being produced." Jason then paused and took a sip of

29

coffee.

To Andy's surprised Jan asked Jason "Andy thinks that when this one was built might make a difference in it's value. Does it?"

"Oh it certainly does. There is an old saying about Steinway pianos. 'Over a hundred years is best.' Essentially that meaning the older, the better. That would be for this one and if it was built between 1896 and 1936 it could be even better, maybe even twice as much as one of a later date. I am guessing this could be one of those but without the serial number it is hard to make sure. With a little research I think we can find out."

Andy was now really starting to feel some concern. This could be real money. He had seen a couple for sale on-line approaching a hundred thousand dollars. It was obvious some one had started renovation as the Action was done and the new strings purchased. Thomas Collins certainly had no interest in it or he would have at least cared for it rather than stashing it in that back corner. It could have been left with Collins by a friend who needed to store it for a while. He wasn't even sure if his auction receipt was sufficient proof of ownership. And the fact that the signature and serial number had been ground off made him question that it might be stolen.

"Jason, what do you make of the ground off name plate and serial number?"

"Good question Andy. I have the same thought that you do."

Jan let out a sigh. "You think it was stolen?"

Both Andy and Jason said, "Maybe."

Jason offered, "That paint job is so old that if it was stolen it was probably at least fifty years ago."

There was a pause in the conversation. It was now after ten and Andy and Jan had both had full days. Andy hadn't been sleeping well the last few nights but the excitement of the evening kept him going. Jason looked as bright eyed as when he had first arrived and he was also on a discovery high but he could see Jan was tiring and that Andy needed sleep.

"This is the most excitement I have had in years. I would really liked to help you bring this piano back to life. I've got no talent as far as woodworking goes but I do know Steinway's. How to do adjustments, tuning and a lot of other little secrets to make them sound and function best."

He looked at Andy, then at Jan and then back at Andy. "Please. Let me be part of this."

CHAPTER 8

Andy and Jan walked Jason to the door. They had discussed their situation a bit more and it was left that a decision would be made in the next few days. That Jason would be part of what ever happened. Both of them had taken an immediate liking to him. His obvious excitement and enthusiasm was infectious and he impressed them both as honest.

They shook hands and Andy offered an invite to visit his studio downtown. It had been a fun and fruitful meeting. After the door closed Jan turned to Andy.

"You want to do it, don't you?"

Andy again felt somewhat trapped. Of course he did but he was unsure whether or when he should tell her what seemed to him was going on between himself and the piano. Even thinking such a thing made him feel foolish and he could only imagine how it would make him look if he tried to explain it to her.

"The short answer is yes. The longer answer is let's think about it. I think the choice is between restoring it or selling it as is. I think there is a lot of money involved but there is also the challenge of taking on such a project. Jason has added some skills that I don't have that were a worry to me."

Andrew's Piano

Jan looked as if that was good enough for now. She even let a small smile show up and let Andy know that it wasn't an absolutely no at the moment. They headed for bed and cuddled up for a goodnight hug and a kiss. In a few minutes Andy could tell Jan was already asleep. How she could do this had always amazed him. Unless he was exhausted it would take him a half hour or more to fall asleep. Tonight it would take a long time.

At breakfast the next morning all was good and the day was starting off as usual. Andy had put the Action back on the work bench in the garage and covered everything up except the big Case. He looked at it again and for the first time noticed that the Soundboard looked good. Cleaned of all the foundry dust the wood looked solid and he couldn't see any cracks. The surface was smooth and didn't appear to have any blemishes. Maybe, he thought, it had also been refurbished. What a break that would be. He looked at the contour but was afraid to touch it. The "New Curve" Model C. Andy smiled.

He was out the house by eight-thirty and Jan left by nine. He had a small fridge at the studio and would most days fix a sandwich for lunch. Usually Jan would take a lunch with her. Sometimes they would meet at home if the timing was good and both tried to be home by five. Jan often had to work a Sunday at an open house for a few hours, and of course had showings to do whenever required, but she could other wise schedule her time anyway she wanted. Andy was almost always on his own schedule. They thought it was a nice way to go about things.

Bill stopped by shortly after Andy arrived at his studio and as usual just walked in. Their studio doors were directly opposite each other across the hall and when at work they were left open. So dropping in unannounced was almost a daily occurrence.

"Okay Andy let me know what's going on. I can see Jan hasn't thrown you out yet. Still romancing a piano?"

"Bill, I have a story to tell you." Andy filled Bill in all on all that had happened in the last twenty-four hours. About contacting Jason Roberts and him verify the piano as a Steinway. That it may be quite valuable.

"Are you going to restore it? What does Jan think about that? How much is the damn thing worth?" Bill's questions came out as one sentence.

"Maybe. Not sure. A lot," Andy replied, laughing. "We have some serious thinking to do about what the next steps are going to be. Jason is a neat guy and is so excited about helping out on this he can hardly wait for me to get started. He owns a vintage Steinway, is a pianist, and knows how to tune one. He's no craftsman so wouldn't be helpful that way but he knows the anatomy, what all the parts do and where to get replacements. Jan is a bit worried about this and we are going to work that out, one way or another. It could be worth a hundred thousand dollars if in perfect condition."

"A hundred thousand! Jesus Andy, that's a lot of money."

"Makes you think about it, doesn't it."

Bill stepped around Andy's sculpture stand and sat down on the guest stool. "Man, and I thought you were totally nuts. Still do, but you got to be kidding me. A hundred thousand."

"Could be, maybe, maybe not. I don't really have

any idea." Andy paused then added, "Bill, don't you go spreading this around. It's okay if everyone thinks I am a bit off my rocker. Leave it that way for now. Please."

"Sure, good buddy, but let me help out if you do it. You will, won't you?"

"Of course I will."

"Are you going to do it?"

Andy paused before answering. He had decided. It was decided. He had no choice but to restore the piano. To find out what was going on with this thing he sensed so clearly when he touched that "New Curve" contour."

"It has been decided." Andy said looking Bill straight in the eyes. "Don't you tell anyone. I mean any-one. Understand."

CHAPTER 9

Andy was applying the last coat of Smooth On, a two part latex rubber molding compound, to the eagle sculpture when Jason Roberts dropped in after he had knocked on the open studio door. "Hi Andy. Have you got a few minutes to talk?"

"Sure Jason. Good to see you. I have to finish up here. It will take about fifteen minutes but we can chat while I work. No way I can make any mistakes at this point." Andy then added, "I should have already gotten back to you but I am trying to get this piece ready to cast and I promised Jan I would get the waxes to the foundry before even looking at the piano again. It's been a rough few days and I have several more of them before I get it done."

"I understand what your saying but you haven't even thought about the piano since I came over last week?" Jason spoke softly and Andy could tell he was disappointed.

"Not exactly. Making the mold is a do and wait project. Lots of time to think while working and more time waiting between coats. Don't tell Jan that I have spent a bit of time thinking over the piano project. And by the way, that was a delightful evening we had last week. I should have called you. I am glad you came by."

Jason seemed to relax and was obviously again ready to talk piano. "I did some research on the Steinway web-site and came up with several interesting items. First, it was after 1905 that Steinway New York stopped producing production Model C's but they did many special order builds. Steinway Hamburg continued a regular production schedule through 1936. I found one 1927 Model C for sale on-line with a serial number of 248947 and a production date of March of that year. I sure wish we could find a number close to that so we would know the approximate year of production. Maybe it was put on at another place or part just as a reference. We will have to keep looking. Another thing is that the Patent Numbers are sometimes located on the Frame's cross members and that would make a positive proof that it is a Steinway if they match. I don't recall seeing any when I was examining the Frame but I have no doubt that it is one and I think it will be New York between 1905 and 1936. The best of the best years "

Andy smiled at that. Jason's enthusiasm filled the studio and he thought it was time to confide in him his not so secret secret. He was now finished applying the last coat of rubber, looking over every square inch to make sure he hadn't missed any spots, and then put the brush in the plastic bowl and set them aside.

"Jason, I will level with you right now. I haven't told Jan yet but she knows me so well I think she is already resigned to it. I am going to do the restoration." Andy pulled his other stool over nearer where Jason was sitting. He had a big grin on his face. "And you are going to be as involved with it as much as you want to be for the entire project. I have no doubt about doing the cabinet work. I can do most of it in the garage and if not there is plenty of talent here in Loveland to get the work done. Bill Holstead, the sculptor next door, will be helping out. He knows, Jan doesn't. Please don't say anything to her until after I tell her."

"Great! I knew you wanted to but I was afraid you might not be able to work it out with your wife. You have no idea how excited I am about this. These are my true loves, music and Steinway pianos."

They talked about planning and how Jason would compliment the early phasing by his knowledge of what was important to do first and what could be done later. Andy suggested he might like to participate in the really dirty work like paint stripping but he indicated he might be just in the way. It wasn't his thing.

Andy then set up a possible schedule. He had four or five days work left to get two sets of waxes of the eagle sculpture to the foundry and another week to complete his two small sculptures. Then he could start on the Case.

"Jason, when you were over to the house last week our garage tour was short and I can't remember if I told you about the two boxes that came with the buy. One box had a number of smaller ones that were imprinted with Genuine Steinway Parts. They contained unopened packets of piano strings. All coiled and different sizes, diameters and weights. I only looked in a couple but it looks like there were lots of them." Jason almost fell off his stool and his eyes bulged. "In the other box was all sorts of stuff. Some more Steinway boxes with pin like bolts. Some red felt ribbons. Lots of stuff, Also the three castors in brass that I can polish up to look like new."

"My God man you are the lucky one. It is looking

more and more like whoever owned that piano had ordered just about everything needed to do the restoration. Maybe everything except the paint remover and the poor soul who has to use it. What does the Soundboard look like? I didn't take close look because my eye had caught the Action and we also were checking out the Frame."

"Well I just happened to, on one of my visits to the garage, take a close look. It looks good. No cracks and no blemishes. Almost like new. I couldn't check the bottom side. You know why. That is one big piece of furniture."

Jason was positively beaming. It was almost hard to look at him. Andy was also smiling.

"I need two more weeks." Andy offered.

The two new friends shook hands and both understood the meaning of what Andy had just said. This was going to an adventure and it was going to be good to have someone to share in it.

CHAPTER 10

The two weeks to finish up what he had promised to Jan seemed to drag along. Andy was tired and trying not to let his mind wander about too much. At special moments when he was home alone he would venture into the garage and look at all the pieces and parts. He had cleared the shelves he had set up to store his more seldom used sculpture tools and supplies, taking them to his studio, and now they were loaded with the piano's inventory. Almost daily, whenever he was up to it, he would place his hand on the contour for reassurance that he wasn't crazy. It was always there, strong and undeniable. It was like an addiction, and maybe it was one. Sometimes in the studio, or even in the middle of the night, a craving occurred that was insatiable. It worried him as he had no idea what was going on. He only knew he had to find out and that meant he had to restore the piano and had to do it perfectly.

He had set up the Action in the living room section of the town home on the small work bench from the garage. The bench was covered with a blanket and didn't show through. The Action was such a marvelous piece it looked like a work of art. It was of course, and it was enjoyable just to look at. When he was alone he would pull up a dinning room chair and admire it for a while and then press a few keys. Sometimes a melody would come to mind and he would play with the keyboard in unison as if he knew what he was doing. He had some kind of a connection with it that he had no understanding. Not like when touching the Case but none the less it gave him comfort. With so much else that was on his mind, he chose not to question what it was. He realized he couldn't tell anyone about this without looking like a fool so he would keep it to himself.

Jan had to be told about the plan to do the restoration. Telling her he was going to do it would be hard to do. Tonight would have to be the night. The waxes were in the foundry. He had finished the two smaller sculptures, made the molds, would be doing the waxes tomorrow and have them in the foundry in a couple days. It was time to start the paint stripping of the Case. The smaller pieces he would do after the Case if that went well. If it was too big of a job there was a local stripping business that could do the legs and the Lyre Post that holds the three pedals, the top covers and the rest of the painted parts. He could easily transport them but the Case would be a major problem to move about. When the Case took up the entire floor of the garage, Jan would know.

She came home at her usual time and seemed in good spirits. That was good, Andy thought. She had just had a contract signed with a quick closing so there would be income in the near future. The casting costs were payment on delivery and if he decided have the metal chasing done by one of the local chasers it would add even more to the production billing. Andy could do it but he had other plans in mind. The gallery in Palm Desert had told him they had sold two of the eagle sculptures from the photographs of the original sculpture he had sent them. As soon as one was ready to ship to their customer they would send the first check. The second sale was contingent with a local collector and he would purchase it when he saw that the bronze lived up to photos of the sculpture in wax. Andy was well aware that in bronze sculpture, unless you are famous, the only way you can make any money is selling in editions. The eagle would be sold in an edition of twenty-five. The real profit didn't arrive until casting number four, or five, was sold when you could have the foundry do full service and your initial time and costs had been recouped.

After dinner Andy started with him saying. "You remember a few days ago I told you about Jason Roberts dropping by the studio?"

"Your are going to do it, aren't you!" Jan cut him off. "I knew you would. It is just too much of a challenge and is just what you really like to do. Isn't it!" But she wasn't through yet and lifted her right hand with her index finger pointing right at him, right between his eyes. "Okay buster, but get this straight and let's be clear about it. If it gets to be too much trouble. Too much time. Too much money. Starts to ruin our life it goes. It goes! Gone!"

Andy's mouth opened, and then closed. Then it did so again. He smiled a somewhat crooked smile and slowly replied. "I think you made it clear enough. I am okay with that. I hope this is the right thing to do. I really do. There is so much that seems right about it that I am sure it will work out. Thank you for knowing me so well. You know you have made much of my life possible. I would never have been here, traveling the road that got me here, without you. You know that."

Jan looked at Andy for a minute, then flushed just a bit. "Okay. Don't go and blow it," she said softly.

Other than give Jan a smile, there wasn't much else Andy could say or do. He thought this has to work. It just has to.

CHAPTER 11

Andy had caught up on his sculpture schedule. The two eagle pieces were in casting, as were the two smaller works, two each, running one week behind. Six walnut bases had been ordered from Colorado Bases on Fourth Street, and the metal chasers and the patina craftsmen scheduled. American Bald Eagle casting number one was put on priority. Andy was committing to a lot of expenses over a short period and the only sure income would be from it's sale.

He now felt the time had come to start the restoration and the first step was to get the garage ready. A piece of black plastic covering most of the floor area was duct taped securely in place to protect it from what may come its way. Next Andy made a rectangular box of three inch plastic pipe, eight by three feet, and wrapped some light weight plastic around it so that it could catch any spilled paint remover and paint when strategically placed under the Case. He constructed two six foot long saw horses that would support the Case at a comfortable working height. Planning on doing the flat side first he arranged the catcher box, with saw the horses in the position such that when the Case was placed top side up it would be under that side.

Bill had come over for the first big lift and he greeted Andy with, "So you are going to do it. You said Jan had okay-ed the project. Wait til she has to go out in the snow to dig her car out at ten degrees with the wind blowing."

"Come on Bill, the Fourth of July is still a week away."

"You think it will done a year from now?" Bill chortled.

"Give me a break and help me lift this thing onto the horses."

The piano was now in place. It looked better, but not much, horizontal. It was big and the garage now seemed smaller. Bill then offered another pearl.

"What are you going to call her? Or him? Or it?"

Andy had never given a thought about that. "Well, no longer the beast, that's for sure. I will have to think about it." He also thought, although it just flashed through his mind, what would the piano liked to be called. Followed immediately by my God, why am I thinking about something like that.

Bill looked around some more and needing to get back to work parted with, "You know, it does have a nice shape. Sort of sexy in a way. Have fun Andy."

"Thanks Bill. You all don't be a stranger, ya hear."

Right then Jason showed up giving Bill a wave as he drove off. "Hi Andy. You've started. Great, Great. Let me look at the bottom before you put the chemicals on."

Jason, with some grunts, got down on the floor on the curve side and slid under. He had his pencil flashlight and started inspecting. He then tapped on the sound board with his knuckles and pretty much went all around the entire edge, Then a few raps in the mid section and crawled out from under. He had a big smile on his face.

"I will say it again, you are one lucky guy. I think it is new or the original totally refurbished. Sounds just right. You won't have to do a thing. After you get the cosmetics done we should be able to string her up."

Andy let out a laugh and a sigh at the same time. "I think I'll take a little time off. Jason let's go inside and talk a bit."

"Sure. What's on your mind?"

They went inside. Andy offered a soft drink but they both settled for glasses of water. He then looked around the room for no real reason and then asked Jason. "Do you know any lawyers you trust? Here's what I am thinking. We need to find out, before we get too far into this project, who started the restoration, where did he get the piano and did he have ownership? Some one has put a lot of money into it. If it was stolen, how much later could it be claimed? Would Thomas Collins have any claim at all or could the IRS get involved? All I have is the auctioneer's little receipt of a hundred dollar payment for piano parts. What do you think?"

"I think I don't have any idea. You do have a bunch of points. I do happened to know a lawyer I trust whose is semi-retired but might actually be able to help. Roberta Roberts, the woman I am currently living with."

"You can trust her?" laughed Andy.

"You bet. Actually her ex-partner is still practicing and they are still good friends. I will have her talk to him, not on chargeable hours mind you, and he can give us an opinion. Even better he likes pianos. If we need to go further I am sure he can advise us which way and how far to go. It's probably a really good idea to find this out."

Andy shifted in his chair. "You know, I am more nervous now, maybe even a little scared, than I have been the entire time this has been going on. It has only been four weeks and it seems like it was a year ago I lifted paddle one sixty-seven."

CHAPTER 12

After Jason had left Andy returned to the piano and started a closer inspection of the Case. The inside looked so much better than the outside and it gave him a boost in confidence. Dampening a towel with just a trace of fine oil he wiped down the entire interior. The Soundboard took on a whole new look as it's lacquered surface, which was in such good condition, had a sheen that had been hidden by dust and grime. The bridge looked almost new and seemed secure. Even the inside of the Case appeared to be in good shape with very few dings and scrapes. It had a little of the white antiquing paint on it but mostly just small drips and spatters. It was a dull black and when the towel cleaned off the residue it actually exposed a glossy black finish under the lacquer. More good news. Again Andy knew that he had really lucked out.

Andy went around the edge of the Soundboard and the side with two inch blue painters tape making sure it was tight to the side. He also decided to tape the top inside of the Case and would deal with the small white paint spatters later. Unrolling some clear plastic and covering the Soundboard he cut it to fit and taped it in place. He did the inside wall in a similar fashion. He wanted to protect the inside from any spills of paint remover.

Andrew's Piano

Pouring some of the remover into a small pot and using a 4 inch paint brush Andy applied a first coat on about a four foot length starting near the front. The paint remover was formulated to stick on vertical surfaces and for the most part it did. The catch box proved it's worth, however.

An hour later Andy came back to survey the results. He was amazed at how the white antiquing paint had reacted to the remover. With just minimal effort it slid off and fell into the catch box. This might not be the grungy job he had expected. Five hours later he had most of white paint off the Case's side and rim. That was enough for the day and as it was a Sunday he would clean himself up and maybe watch whatever golf tournament was on TV. Jan was doing an open house at one of the more expensive homes on the market and would be home soon. It was also a very nice day outside and Andy thought it has been too long since he had done anything other than work on his sculpture or on the piano. It was strange that he didn't really feel tired. He tried to concentrate on the golf match but he quickly lost interest. He had just turned the television off when Jan got home.

"How was it?"

"Okay. I had a pretty good number come through and I may have a new client. A nice young couple moving here from Boston, Massachusetts of all places. He is going to work at Hewlett Packard and she is, get this, a classical pianist and will be teaching music at Loveland High School. Nice kids. They want me to put together some properties to show so I will be busy next week. It's a nice house and shows well. I wouldn't be surprised if they may end up choosing it. You are all cleaned up. How did your day in the garage go?"

Jan had actually asked the question with interest and Andy was pleased about that. "I had a good day, too. First the Soundboard is in great shape, just as Jason thought. He knows more about that than me but what I like is that it looks like all I have to do is give it a couple of coats of lacquer and it will shine. Even better, the white paint was easy to remove and underneath are coats of lacquer over black paint that looks like it may also be good. I can't be sure until I thoroughly clean off paint remover residue but that will be a really big benefit if it doesn't have to stripped back to the wood." Then he added. "Maybe I can actually do this."

"What do you mean, maybe?" was Jan's quick and good natured reply.

Jan then suggested to Andy why didn't they go to Adelita's for dinner tonight and invite Jason and his wife.

"Great idea. Where's the phone?"

"Where it always is."

It was there, of course, and Andy got out Jason's number and made the call. He answered and the invitation was extended and quickly accepted.

Then Andy asked Jason another question. "Do you two play bridge?"

Jason was quick to answer. "Yes we do."

"How about coming over to our place for desert and play a little bridge after dinner?"

Andy could hear Jason repeat the question to Roberta and then clearly heard her say, "We would love to." They would meet at the restaurant at the five-thirty opening time.

"They play bridge!" Jan was now one happy wife.

Bridge was her favorite game and it had been some time since they had found another couple that played. She looked at Andy and said, "You did that all your own. Maybe that piano is working some kind of magic on you."

Andy put on a good smile but knew that the day was coming when she would have to know that the magic that the piano had over him was not exactly what she was just now thinking.

Adelita's didn't disappoint and dinner was both good and fun. A couple of margaritas didn't hurt either. Both Andy and Jan had their first chance to meet Roberta and she was a cheerful and attractive lady. She and Jason made a perfect couple. Andy and Jan both thought they may make very good friends and hoped that would happen. Really good friends are hard to come by and it was to turn out they would need them in the near future.

CHAPTER 13

After the Roberts had left Jan came over to Andy and put her arms around him. "They are really nice. I like them both and this was a really fun evening." It was a good feeling of closeness that had been missing for some time. The stress of last years move to Loveland and essentially starting over at their age had been a little more than either had anticipated. The entrance of the piano had amplified it. Jan gave Andy a kiss and lead him to the bedroom. It was a one of the best nights that Andy could remember having in some time and helped him sleep soundly all night.

When the Roberts first came in the door after the dinner at Adelita's Jan announced that the boys could have exactly five minutes in the garage while she put on the coffee and set up the bridge table. "Five minutes only! Understand!"

Both Andy and Jason had heard and understood the command as they entered the garage. Roberta turned to Jan and commented, "Just like little boys playing with a new toy. Jason is so excited about the project I hope he doesn't try to move into your guest room. He has needed something like this ever since he retired."

Jan thought this over and realized that she and

Andrew's Piano

Andy needed someone like the Roberts too. She felt good about this.

The bridge went as the rest of the evening had. Fun, relaxed and social. The Roberts were good players but did not take the game too seriously. Mistakes were overlooked, questions could be answered, and even better, the cards were good for both sides.

Between rubbers Roberta offered a little on the ownership question that Andy had discussed with Jason. She said she did not have much to offer yet. She had discussed it with her former associate, Ben Halpern. He didn't think there would be much recourse for any later claim of previous ownership because of the timing and the IRS's right to claim the contents of the foundry. The prior auction notices published were to notify anyone claiming ownership of any of the contents to make a claim and remove anything successfully challenged before the auction date.

She also said the had found one item of interest on a site that lists stolen property records. The Broadmoor Hotel in Colorado Springs went into receivership in 1937. On a list of property involved there was a 1928 Steinway Grand Piano itemized as missing. Curious.

The next morning was a good one for the Miller's. Jan was happy and Andy had slept all night. After a good breakfast Jan was off to work and Andy was in the garage.

He picked out a stiff bristled scrub brush and attacked the Case rubbing off all the dried up residue of the paint remover. Once he had it cleaned off he switched to his electric orbital sander with 220 grit paper and carefully started to sand the exposed lacquered surface. After covering about half the flat side of the Case he made a detailed inspection. The surface was smooth. There were no scrapes, dents or chips on the underlying wood. He took his oiled cloth and wiped away the dust from the sanding and there appeared a beautiful ebony black finish. He then hooked up his trouble light and toured the entire Case. There were no visible scratches, dents, cracks, or dings anywhere. It was almost, or even was, perfect.

Andy sat down on his workbench stool and looked at his hands. "What is going on?" he said out loud. "I just don't understand this." Then another thought started to formulate. He went over to the piano and ran his hand along the contoured portion of the Case and the sensation he was craving started to be sensed and the thought crystallized. The white antique paint was camouflage. It wasn't for any kind of stage look. It was just camouflage. Who would want or even look at a piano that was so ugly? The finish under that awful stuff was perfect. The heavy brush strokes and the streaks of gold antiquing would hide any sight of a perfect finish.

It was then time to take a closer look at the rest of the painted pieces. Andy could see that there were no cracks or deep scratches on them. There were no dings or dents. How had the piano gone through so many years without major damage? Or had it been restored to this state including new finishing and then painted and stored somewhere eventually ending up in that back corner of Collins's foundry? Who had done this and when? Was it in the 1950's, before World War Two, or just before it was to be stored in the foundry?

Andy again rubbed the contour surface and felt the comfort and confident feeling he so desperately needed. "Lucky me."

Andrew's Piano

He hadn't been to his studio for over a week and decided to go there and touch base with Bill. Opening his door to his studio he thought he smelled something, like a wisp of perfume, in the hallway. Bill's door was closed so he stepped across and knocked on it with a little robust staccato. In a moment the door opened and a young, very feminine face with the prettiest blue eyes you have ever seen said, "Hi".

"And you are?"

She laughed a nice laugh and in a equally nice voice introduced herself as Julia Anderson from Maine. Andy was lost for words. The door had opened some more and the rest of Julia matched up very well with her face and Andy now knew the source of the perfume.

"Does Bill Holstead still live here?" Andy asked and Julia's laughter brightened the day even more.

CHAPTER 14

The next several weeks were going to be tough for Andy. His goal was to strip and sand all the piano's painted surfaces and prepare them for several finishing lacquer applications, the last one after all the other work was completed.

Seeing Bill at the studio the morning after meeting Miss Julia from Maine was a treat. Bill was blushing when he explained that she had been a former girl friend who had called a few days earlier saying she wanted to be a current one and could she come to see him in Loveland. Bill told Andy that it took all of one minute after she showed up at his studio door to fall head over heels in love with her again. She had been here three days and he had got nothing done since but had never been happier. There was nothing Andy could say to that so he changed the subject.

"Bill, I have a proposition for you. If you could manage a few hours a week for the next couple of months could you monitor my casting schedule? This would be to follow the scheduling, do inspections, check on the metal chasing and patina, see the basing gets done right and do shipping for me. I only have six pieces going and the first eagle casting should be out of the foundry in the next few days. That's the money piece. You are using all the same people so you shouldn't have problems that way. The piano is going to be full time until it is playable and it is going to take a couple of months."

Bill thought this over. He wasn't worried about Andy paying him. He had done some work for him before and was always treated fairly. "Sure, no problem."

There was an awkward pause then Bill continued. "I'd like you and Jan to get to know Julia. She is really a nice person. Fun to be around and she will need some friends here beside me. You can understand."

"You bet. We have just gotten to know Jason and Roberta Roberts a little and I think, although you and Julia are a lot younger, you both would like them. Jan has a new young couple as clients, says they seem really nice and are about Julia's age. Maybe we can plan a small party and get everyone together. I will talk to Jan and see if we can put it together. Maybe this week end. I am thinking that this could become Team Piano. When the piano is done we will throw a really big party."

Bill face broke into a broad smile. "Your are okay, amigo," he said as he rushed back to his studio and to who was there.

Andy headed back home and into the garage. The real effort was now underway. Over the next few weeks it would take three gallons of paint remover, many brushes, lots of plastic, blue tape, and sand paper. And when he was done a garage that would be ready for a complete cleaning with all the piano parts cleaned and ready for the their final coats of lacquer.

It was as Andy started this part that he discovered that one piece was missing. It was called the Pin Block. It wasn't that it needed paint removal, it was that it was a very important piece that would have to be crafted to very precise tolerances. It required a special wood which would have to be ordered, carefully shaped and fitted and then accurately drilled with some 228 holes. This was the first set back to what otherwise had been a very easy restoration to this point with the many time and money saving discoveries. Andy was sure he hadn't missed it in the foundry as it was an odd shaped piece, almost four feet long, having all those holes. He was sure he could make one but he hoped Jason would have a better solution.

Andy called Jason but it was Roberta who answered the phone. Jason was out but he would call as soon as he got back. She of course told Andy again how much Jason enjoyed being involved. It did Andy good to have someone with his enthusiasm always ready to lend a hand. Once the piano was ready to string he would be indispensable.

An hour later Jason called back. When Andy told him about the missing Pin Block he said "How could I not have seen that it was missing? It's where all the tuning pins are. When tuning the piano you have your nose down into that bed of pins, going back and forth for hours. It is one of the very most important parts."

"Do you know where we can order the block of wood? I understand that is a very special laminate of five or more pieces with each piece having the grain at a different angle." replied Andy.

"You got that part right. I think our best bet is to order the block directly from Steinway. It will be pretty expensive. We may be able to get them to send a pattern for the Model C. They may want the year. Hopefully not the serial number. The block is fitted to the under side of the Frame so we could work from that point. It has to fit perfectly. Your are an engineer. You can figure it out."

Jason was so eager to help he volunteered to call Steinway that afternoon, even though it might be too late in New York and he would probably have to wait until tomorrow. Then he offered that he knew a restorer in Indiana that might be of help and he could also try him.

"That will be great, Jason. We will figure it out."

"I have no doubt about it, Andy."

CHAPTER 15

Andy was back in the garage looking over what he had learned was called the piano's Belly. It seemed a rather crude term for such a dramatic, or soon to be, space when everything was in it's place. He then looked where the missing Pin Block should be located. It suddenly dawned him that what he thought was a panel that the Pin Block should sit on was actually a veneered L shaped cover held in place by a number of small screws. It had the same gray appearance as the inside sides of the Case so he had not paid much attention to it. Running his fingers under the front edge he felt an unusual shape and knew immediately what it was. "Stupid me, stupid me," he muttered to himself as he got a small screwdriver and removed the six screws. Lifting the cover off there was one beautiful sight. A drilled Pin Block, obviously fitted and mounted and ready to fulfill it's purpose.

He ran back into the house and grabbed the phone and punched Jason's number and when he answered, before Andy could say anything, Jason was talking.

"New York was already closed for the day and I had to leave a message at my friend's in Indiana. You just called me fifteen minutes ago for crying out loud."

"Jason! Stupid me! I just found the Pin Block. It is

right where it should be looking so new you would think it was installed an hour ago. And it is drilled. It is ready. It is beautiful."

"What are you. . . . . " Jason got that far, paused and then finished, "You got to be kidding me. Your joking?"

"You said it before. I am one lucky guy."

"I will be there in ten minutes," and he hung up.

Jason made it in nine minutes and was breathing hard when he came through the door. "Let me see it!" had the two of them pushing and shoving each other into the garage. Jason hustled around the piano until he could see the Pin Block and almost started to cry. "It's beautiful." He ran his hand over the entire surface. "Have you a bottle of wine? How about a toast to good fortune?"

Andy went into the kitchen and returned with two glasses and a bottle of wine. The two friends clinked glasses and with a nod to the Pin Block took a substantial swig. It wasn't a great wine but it tasted great. Andy went over to the shelves where he had all the small parts stored and returned to Jason's side. He set the Genuine Steinway Parts box labeled "250 Tuning Pins" on the Pin Block and they had a second toast.

Pulling up the stools they sat where they could look into the Belly and see the Pin Block. Andy then told Jason about the Case and all the rest of the parts being in such good shape that he didn't think he would have to completely strip them down and repaint. It was such good news that another toast was in order. He then explained his theory that they had been painted the ugly antique white as camouflage.

"Andy, that makes a lot of sense. Whoever was doing the restoration was pretty close to completing it and must have had to give it up for some reason. Painting it like that would most likely keep prying eyes at bay, especially it being in parts like you found it. I wonder what happened? How long ago?"

"I wonder who it was? I am not sure I want to find out," Andy answered.

Just then Jan made an entrance and asked to join the boys club. Jason jumped up, almost spilling the remainder of the wine in his glass, to offer his seat. Andy smiled and brought in a chair from the dining room and a second trip for a glass and poured some for her. "You are from this minute on a member of the Andrew's Piano Boys Club. Welcome."

They clinked glasses and sat in the garage next to the Steinway Model C. It seemed to be one of those times where nothing much needed to be said. There was the start of a mess in the garage and it would be getting worse as the paint stripping proceeded but at this moment it felt as this was the place they should be. The three of them were comfortable with each other and the piano. None of them had any real idea what was in store but for whatever reason it was a nice time to have a glass of wine together and look forward to the future.

Later Jan said to Andy "That was nice out there in the garage. There is something about that big piano on the saw horses just waiting to be restored that has an appeal. I don't know how to describe it. I just sense it. You and Jason know. I can tell that. Can you tell me what it is?"

Andy had to think for a minute. This wasn't what he was experiencing when he touched the piano, but he knew what Jan was asking. "When there is a thing worth

Andrew's Piano

doing, and you can do it, it is almost like a commandment that you make the effort. The final object here is that when this piano is restored it will again be a beautiful example of man's creativity and inventive skill. When it is played by a true pianist it will provide the music that is a necessary part of the human condition. For me it is that I want to be a part of something akin to saving a life. Much of the work has already been done by someone else, and I am only finishing what was started, but it needs to be done. Why fate picked me I have no idea but I am glad it has happened. I want to hear the music."

Jan gave Andy a questionable look but seemed satisfied. She finished her wine and told Andy she would go fix dinner. "Half an hour?" Andy sat there, staring at nothing, nodded okay.

CHAPTER 16

It was a very good three weeks for all of the team members. The team was not formally organized yet but had informally grown to eight. Andy, Jan, Bill, Jason and Roberta, and new additions Julia Anderson and Ron and Stefanie Stevens. The Stevens's were the newest addition. They were the young couple just arrived from Boston and they had quickly decided on the house Jan had on open house just a few weeks earlier. Their offer was made and accepted and as Jan had both sides of the transaction it would be a good payday for her. More important than that was that Stefanie was a classical pianist and the discussion of the restoration of the Steinway Model C was of immediate interest to her. Adding to that was that Ron was an engineer and looked to be not only smart but strong. Julia was already becoming a friend, and at the party at Andy and Jan's two days previous had struck a bond with the Stevens. Suddenly it seemed a team had formed.

Jan had proposed they have a party and the planning had started. Andy had finished all the paint removal much faster than he had anticipated and was getting the garage cleaned up. A big bundle of plastic was carted over to the studio and placed in the big dumpster in the alley. The shop-vac ran for over an hour as the fine sanding of the lacquer had left a coating of dust on everything in the garage. He had taken the metal parts over to George Patterson's and rented some chasing bench time. With his air tools and polishing pads he soon had the brass taking on a gold appearance and looking fantastic.

Andy decided to mount the legs on the case and would do the final lacquering with them in place. He found the big lag bolts in the parts box and after attaching the the casters to the legs mounted them. He did the forward leg first by lifting the Case up slightly, blocking it enough to give clearance. Once the leg was attached he was able remove the forward saw horse. He repeated the procedure for the remaining two legs, one at a time. With a little help from Jan he was then able to remove the second saw horse and the piano Case was on it's own legs and looking like it should.

While this was going on Jan was busy organizing the party. As space in the town home was somewhat limited it was going to be a buffet with lots of finger food and several special dishes with only a single fork necessary menu. The refrigerator would be stocked with beer and soft drinks and two big bottles of wine on the counter. It was planned to be around late afternoon on Friday. The weather would co-operate with a beautiful Colorado afternoon.

By the time the first guest arrived Andy and Jan were ready and anxious to see how this new group would mix. Jason and Roberta were the senior citizens, Andy and Jan the middle aged, and Bill followed by a few years by Julia and the Stevens, the youngsters. From the first minute when all had arrived the mix was such that you thought all had been friends for years. Jan's happy expression told Andy that all was well in his world right now. One could sense true friendships were being made. Andy thought "These are good people. These are ones who you want for your friends."

Before attacking the food everyone, with drinks in hand, went into the garage. All standing around the piano and quietly chatting about music, pianos, piano playing, singing and performing. Jason was a good pianist and it turned out Stephanie had majored in classical piano in college and spent a year at Julliard. She said she was on the edge to turn professional but smart enough to know how hard it would be to make a living that way. She pointed out she didn't want to end up playing in hotel lobbies. She would be happy for now teaching music at the high school level. Julia surprised all by letting it be known that she was a singer and had been in a number of off Broadway musicals in New York. She hadn't been happy there and decided time with Bill might be a better choice. She smiled a big smile while saying that.

Back inside Andy turned on the stereo with his five disc CD player loaded with Dave Brubeck's Time Out, Erroll Garner's Concert by the Sea, a disc having a piano solo of Gershwin's *Rhapsody in Blue*, another CD of Debussy favorites having *Clair de lune*, and even a CD featuring Rachmaninoff's *Piano Solo Concerto No2*. The player was set on random shuffle and the volume low enough to allow for good conversation. It seemed to be a good selection for the group.

Some time shortly after dessert was served and most were in comfortable conversations Andy went out to the garage and put his hands on the piano, opposite the contour side. He could sense some sensation, but it was not strong. His mind was not really focused on it. He just felt good. He had been able to suddenly be surrounded by a group of people who he could think of as real friends. It had been some time since he had friends like these. Jan had been his best friend since the day he first met her, and Bill was a new one, but other than those two most other people he new and liked were just friendly acquaintances.

Andy heard someone close ask, "Can you feel it too?" It startled him, both that someone was there and by the question. He turned toward the voice and it was Stefanie standing close to him with her hands on the rim. She seemed to be doing just what he was doing. Touching a partially restored piano while music was drifting in from the living room. He asked "What are you feeling?"

"I am not sure. The music, the making of new friends in a new place, touching what will become a wonderful piano. It is a really good feeling. Thank you for making it happen."

CHAPTER 17

Andy spent the next day converting the garage into the paint shop. This meant hanging plastic on the walls with overlaps at the door into the house and making a curtain across the garage door with an opening for an exhaust system to the outside. With the garage door open the ceiling had a cover that could be lifted into place. It was simple but would be sufficient to exhaust most of the fumes from the lacquer spraying and protect the walls and ceiling from over spray. Filters at both the exhaust and inlet would keep the air somewhat clear. A drawback was that it couldn't be used if the wind was blowing, any of the neighbors were home or their cars were near by. The piano case and legs were completely covered and would be done last.

His first spray day was very successful and all the smaller pieces got their first coat with no complaints from the neighbors, most likely because they were not home. The lacquer required two days to harden so he had some down time. Andy decided it was time to see if he could trace how the piano had ended up in Thomas Collins's foundry. The first step was to contact the reclusive Collins.

Andy started by talking to George Patterson as he knew almost all the sculptors in the area. George didn't have any direct information but he thought Collins was living south of Colorado Springs and had heard he might be casting some pieces in one of the foundries in the area. A few calls and Andy had a lead in that he was casting and selling under the alias, Collin West. Trying several galleries he found a gallery owner in La Veta that was representing him. The owner was reluctant to give out his phone number as might be expected. Andy explained that he had no interest in buying any of West's sculpture and that the reason he wanted to talk to him had to with that he had bought an item at the IRS auction at Thomas Collins's foundry a few months back and he might have information about it. The gallery owner said he would pass on Andy's phone number but doubted Collin West would respond.

Less than an hour later Andy's phone rang and immediately after his hello he heard.

"This is Collin West. Who am I talking to and what do you want?"

It was not an unfriendly voice but certainly not one eager for conversation. Andy spoke slow and introduced himself.

"Hi. My Name is Andy Miller. I am sculptor up here in Loveland. A few weeks ago at the IRS auction at Thomas Collins's foundry I was the high bidder on a group of piano parts. Might you have any information about them?"

"Maybe," was answered without any commitment.

"If I could talk to Thomas I would like to know how they ended up in that corner behind the big boiler. I am thinking of restoring the piano and would like to find out the make, model and any of it's history I can get."

West's quick answer was, "I may know something

about it but it was not mine, never was."

Andy wasn't sure how to take this so decided to take a different tack. "Something I found interesting at that auction was, other than the actual casting floor equipment, how little of value there was in the building. The office furniture, work benches, a few chasing tools, very old and used welding outfit. What caught my eye was that were no master molds for Thomas Collins's sculptures."

There was a loud good natured laugh and West replied. "Since you picked up on that I will talk to you. First understand that as soon as I hang up, this conversation never took place. Do you understand that?"

"I sure do."

"Okay." West paused and then continued, "This is how that piano ended up where you found it. I had the foundry up and running for about a year and was casting a few pieces for Brandon Kellerher when he came in and ask me if I could store a piano for him for a few months. It was in parts and wouldn't take up too much space. He was in some financial straights, was having some medical problems, and had lost his rental space including his garage. He looked so beaten down I said sure and showed him the spot behind the boiler, right where you found it. He told me he had inherited it from his father after he died. His father had started to restore it and Brandon thought he should try to finish it up. He said he had most of the parts he needed but then had to stop working on it as his problems began to mount. He brought it up from Colorado Springs on an open flat bed trailer. A couple of my boys unloaded it for him and stacked it against the wall. It hasn't been moved or touched in the 7 years I had the foundry. That damn Brandon died of pancreatic cancer three months after he dropped it off. I just never even thought to take a look at it. It just became a dust covered part of the wall."

Andy tried to hide his excitement, thanking West politely and started to end the conversation that never occurred by asking how things were going for him.

"Andy, your are okay. Things are real good for me right now and I still have a number of those editions left to cast and sell which helps out a lot. You get my drift. How dumb can the government be."

They both had a good laugh at that and the goodbyes were made.

Andy had half the story. The rest was easily found on line in the brief obituary of Deacon Kellerher who died in 1964 survived by his only child, Brandon Kellerher. He had worked for thirty two years as a maintenance man at the Broadmoor Hotel in Colorado Springs, Colorado.

CHAPTER 18

The paint booth was in full swing as Andy was sanding, spraying, then sanding and spraying again. On the third cycle the individual parts took on a beautiful ebony black finish that was mirror like on the surface. The look is referred to as piano black finish and it was time to call it done. The Case was moved to the center of the work space and the procedure worked it's magic on the Case and the legs as well. Andy was delighted as the painting had been a major worry and was now completed.

There was one last major piece to give attention to and that was the Frame. The gold color was not quite good enough to match up with the rest of the piano. Bill and Ron came over to help Andy position it on the saw horses. At over two hundred pounds it was not that easy to handle, even with the aid of the automobile engine hoist Andy had borrowed from a friend. When it was in place a good sanding followed by spraying of two coats of a lacquer laced with gold bronze powder, and two more coats of clear lacquer, left it glowing with the accepted rich color in the Grand Piano tradition.

It had taken over 3 weeks to get all the finish work done and then the paint booth was disassembled. All the piano parts were now in full display in the now uncluttered garage and it was time to start putting everything to-gether.

During painting Andy found he had quite a lot of spare time. He had lost interest in sculpture and as Bill had been seeing to his casting schedule he was not really too troubled by that. He found he suddenly had a craving to listen to music. Piano music. He set up his stereo system in the garage and would play a single CD over and over listening to how each note was played and the combinations of notes that made up the cords. Occasionally he would put his hands on the piano where he would get the sensation, of the music seeming to come from the Case into his hands, up his arms and into his chest. He felt he could identify each note however complex the playing was and sometimes would think that he was actually doing the playing. This was becoming habitual and he tried to only fall into this world when he felt safely alone.

Hearing the music increased his desire to some how play it himself. He would seat himself in front of the Action and press on the keys not having any idea what the sound would be if the hammers were actually striking the strings. He felt foolish doing this but it was so gratifying he couldn't stop. Returning to the restoration would draw him out of this dream like condition but at every opportunity when having some free time he would be back. It scared him that he couldn't seem to be able to just walk away and he didn't want Jan, or anyone else, to know what was going on.

The entire group came over to watch the Frame lowered into the Case. This had to be carefully done as any slight misalignment could cause a major scratch or scar in the Case's now beautiful finish. With all sides tended Andy slowly lowered the frame by releasing the hydraulic fluid pressure with the small valve on the engine hoist. All went as planed and the golden Frame nestled into it's position flawlessly. It looked fantastic. Nothing but smiles, hugging and clapping when the hoist was moved away and Andrew's Piano stood on it's own, albeit still not complete.

Jason and Roberta took on the hosting of the next team party and each arrived promptly at their home. Walking into their living room the first and dominate thing seen was Jason's antique Steinway Grand, a late 1880's model inherited via three generations. It was a beautiful piano and immaculately maintained. After a nice cocktail hour of conversation and then dinner, there was entertainment that turned out to be a fine few hours of enjoyment and revelation.

Jason had played a few nice pieces during cocktails which had blended in with the conversation. Ron and Stefanie were loving their new home and both happy with their jobs. Bill and Julia were still madly in love and loving life. Julia had hired on to be a teacher's assistant for Stefanie at Loveland High School and Bill had managed to get back to his work at sculpture, his most recent work a fabulous bust of a very attractive young lady. Roberta seemed to be particularly happy as Jason was having such a good time helping Andy. Jan was also a happy lady with new friends, a more interesting social life, and having a very productive few months in real estate sales. Andy was Andy but he knew something was going on that none of the others had any inkling of and was hoping that it would remain that way.

It was after dinner that things really came together.

Jason asked Stefanie if she would like to play the Steinway and she jumped at the chance. Arranging the bench she then set out playing a medley of Broadway show tunes. While she did this she looked at Julia and asked, "Come over here and let's put on a show."

Julia quickly stepped over next to the piano and off the two of them went with Julia singing in a voice so good that it surprised them all. The songs ranged from *Show Me* from My Fair Lady to *Don't Cry For Me Argentina* from Evita. That such young people could be that talented and read their audience so well had tears running down Jan and Roberta's cheeks and even Bill was speechless, damp about the eyes and bursting with pride. Ron knew the quality of Stefanie's playing but was amazed by Julia's voice. All in the room could sense this was something special and Jason was overjoyed that it was taking place in his home. Andy, however, was gripped by a fear he had never experienced before. He now desperately, desperately wanted to be able play his piano. It was almost a panic

Art Myers

CHAPTER 19

The Frame was now secure as the many screws, bolts, special fasteners, along with the two nose bolts that held the Frame to the lower cross beams were all in place. The Pin Block holes were perfectly aligned with their corresponding holes in the Frame. Andy had spent the better part of the day driving the small pins into the Bridge that guide and place the strings on it. Also he positioned in eighty eight agraffe's which with the bridge pins determine the speaking length of the strings.

Jason arrived and he brought the strings that he had taken home to sort out such they would be in order for placement. He told Andy it was a pretty easy job as once he went through the first box for the treble strings he realize they were placed in order already. In the little box that had the selection of small tools was the one used to make the initial winding on the tuning pin, a punch to seat the pin into its hole in the Pin Block, and a small metal mallet. There were other small tools, one for making the twist of the wire about the hitch pins on the Frame, and several for seating and adjusting the positions of the strings.

Jason told Andy he had only done this operation once before and that they should work slowly so as not to make any mistakes. He had brought some spare strings with him and they would practice with them but would not seat the tuning pins as this might damage the hole in the pin block. Several tries were done and soon they both became comfortable with the tools and making the proper looking connections. Andy stood opposite Jason as he slid the first string through the agraffe guide and had Andy bend the end of the wire around the hitch pin and make the bend to secure it. Jason then pulled it tight across the proper Pin Block hole and using this point threaded it in the hole in the pin. He made three wraps around the pin and placed it in the Pin Block hole and gave it a couple of whacks with the mallet seating the pin to about three quarters. String number one was in place.

There were three strings for each key for all of the treble and tenor sections and two and one in the long base strings. It was a big job and took several days to complete. Both Andy and Jason were tired, their hands and fingers hurting, when Jason suggested his friend in Indiana might be someone they should ask to help. That there was a lot of tweaking of the Action and the first tuning could be difficult requiring some expertise that neither of them possessed. Andy thought that might be a very good idea. He had come to the conclusion that what he could do by himself, what had been the original thought, was now mostly accomplished. That he better find at least a little bit of help on what now needed to be done. Actually, quite a bit of help.

That afternoon Jason called back. "Andy, help is on the way. Steve Pardee will be here day after tomorrow and will help us finish with the strings and the Action. He's an expert. He told me he couldn't stand hearing about all the fun I was having and dearly wanted to be a part of it."

"Sounds great Jason. I have come to the conclusion that I do need some help, even more than all you have given me. How is he going to get here and will he be staying at your place?"

"Andy you are so damn lucky. Steve and his wife are old friends of Roberta and me and they will be with us for as long as they want. Steve is a pilot and built his own plane. A beautiful four seat RV10 experimental. Any excuse to fly somewhere is of paramount importance for him and he will fly right into Loveland airport."

"Jason you are some kind of friend. You are right, I am one lucky guy."

Steve Pardee and his wife Sandra arrived as scheduled. They were the same age as Jason and Roberta and just as likable. Enthusiasm would be a good description, so much so that their first stop after landing and having the plane tended was to Andy's garage. Steve fell in love at first sight with the Model C. He almost ran around it twice before reaching in and plucking several strings at random. A smile crossed his face and he then spotted the Action on the work bench and started hitting the keys.

"My God this is beautiful. Just beautiful!"

Andy thought he might hurt himself if he smiled any harder. The five of them then started to laugh together. He wished Jan was here. This was contagious and he wanted her to also be infected.

Steve then turned to Andy. "You know you have something special here, I mean really special. Just those few strings I plucked had a sound and tone so pure that only the most rare pianos, even Steinways, have it. I can hardly wait to get started. We will be making wonderful music before you know it. Can I start tomorrow?"

"The door is open, Steve. You are part of the team. I think what I will be doing is just watching and learning and trying to stay out of the way. Welcome to Loveland."

CHAPTER 20

Jason and Steve were in the garage first thing in the morning. Neither could hide their excitement. Steve had a rolled up leather case which he laid on the work bench next to the Action. He then toured the piano, this time slowly looking and touching everything in sight. He tapped all the tuning pins, the agraffes, bridge pins, ran his finger across the hitch pins, and numerous other points of his interest. He then plucked a few strings at random with his index finger nail. He turn to Andy and Jason. "This looks really good. You two did a fine job. I'm surprised. Almost professional. The finishing is as good as it gets. Maybe a professional could have got a finer finish but yours has something about it that's just a little different. It looks great."

Andy smiled and Jason gave him a poke in the ribs with an even bigger smile.

"Thanks, I appreciate your opinion," was Andy's response. At that moment he needed a positive reaction to his effort. He was also thinking that it may be worth going through this strange obsession he was experiencing just in order to complete the restoration.

Jason was more than happy to add that he thought Andy had done a great job so far and that they had actually strung the piano in a suitable manor. Steve picked up his rolled tool kit and unrolling it exposing a collection of fine tools. "Let's get started."

Steve, with Andy's help, slid the Action into place and secured it with the Key Blocks. He then started by pressing each key from treble to base and back down again.

"It is not that far out of tune. I would have expected it to be way off. Jason, you have always had a good ear so I guess I shouldn't have been that surprised. Also the hammers are so close to being aligned. A couple of days should have this ready if you two don't try to help too much."

"Do you want us to leave you alone. You know, come back tomorrow night to see if your finished?" Andy teased.

"No, no, no! You will want to see how this done. It's not brain surgery but it does take skill and patience. You do need a good ear, however. Right Jason?"

Jason nodded and Andy smiled. He went into the house and brought three card table chairs and set them up. "Anyone coffee, soft drink, water?"

There were no takers and Steve made the first tightening of a string and the A440 tuning was under way by his pressing on the A above middle C key. Another strike and a very slight adjustment, so slight Andy couldn't see the movement but it did sound just a bit different.

At noon a break was deemed necessary and Steve had indicated it would be a good time. Jan had come home for lunch, looked in on the boys and then made up some sandwiches. She met Steve for the first time and again thought what a good group was forming around this piano.

The rest of the afternoon was spent on the tuning. Steve indicated that things were going good and that tomorrow he would work on the Action. He didn't think it would need much work but he could already detect some effort would be required. Other things he mentioned were damper adjustments, some positioning of additional felt, string alignment, hammer alignment, softening of a number of the hammers, something called voicing and regulation.

Then it would be time for playing. A lot of playing and before he returned home one more tuning. Steve was positive about this piano. He didn't speak to Andy or Jason but there was something special about it. It's tone. Even not completely set up yet it had a magnificent tone that he had heard only a few times in his life. He also wanted to be a part of this piano's future.

Jason suggested Adelita's for tonight's dinner and the date was set. Andy and Jan found Steve's wife, Sandra, charming as it seemed all were who they met in this adventure. Half way through dinner Bill and Julia came in and the seating was quickly rearrange for them to join the group. It was decided a playing should happen the next evening. Ron and Stefanie were contacted and they would be there.

By late afternoon the next day Steve said he was finished. The three new friends toasted with cold beers sitting down and spending a few minutes of silence taking in the scene in the garage. It was time to just relax and appreciate the sight of such a beautiful object.

After about half an hour Steve asked, "How about we finish the job?"

"Yes!" answered Andy and Jason in unison.

Andrew's Piano

The Key Blocks were now in place and Andy had mounted the Lyre post and Pedal Box some time ago. It was time to mount the Lid and working together both the rear and front boards were hinged and in place. The Prop was in place and the Lid raised. The Key Slip was next and then the Fallboard. When the Music Rack was in place Andrew's Piano was now whole.

A second beer was ordered and it was a sight to see three grown men show the emotion of the moment with no embarrassment.

Shortly after six the "team" were all present and in the garage standing around the piano. It was beautiful and seemed that for a while each were lost in their own thoughts. It was time for it to be played. After a bit of you first between Jason and Stefanie it was Jason deferring to the better pianist asking her to do the honors.

It was then remembered that there was no bench. A dinning room chair was quickly brought in and Stefanie managed to get comfortable and position her hands. The first sounds from Andrew's Piano were of Debussy's *Clair de lune* filling the garage with sound that everyone there would remember the rest of their lives.

Andy was shaken. It wasn't the sound, the tone or the music, it was that some one else was playing his piano. It wasn't jealousy or envy, it was a fear of losing the connection he had with this beautiful and remarkable instrument.

CHAPTER 21

As Stefanie played *Clair de lune* the group fell into a deep silence, as if a spoken word or even a audible breath would spoil the mood. It seemed to be so perfect in sound, tone and performance that one should solely concentrate on the moment. Stefanie knew in the first minute that something was special with this piano. She seemed to sense that the movement of her fingers on the keys would be perfect and she could concentrate on playing without concern with her fingering. It was the best she had ever played and it seemed to be effortless.

When Stefanie finished all in the garage were silent. There was no need for applause or congratulation. Those who knew classical piano knew they had just heard something exceptional and all that was needed was to savor it. Even those who weren't aficionados also knew that this was special.

Just as the mood might be broken Stephanie struck the first familiar notes and chords of Gershwin's *Raphasody in Blue* and for the next dozen minutes it was spellbinding. As she finished, still with fire, tears were streaming down her face. She knew how good she was playing. How good she might have been or maybe could be. After the final notes were struck she stood and called out to Ron who was at her side in two steps. "Hold me tight for a few minutes. I am scared. Ron, I have never played that good. Never have I been able to play like that. Never." She was uncontrollably crying in his arms.

The rest of the group now understood that something had happened in that garage that was way beyond the normal bounds of the playing of a piano. Jason knew, Julia knew, and Steve knew that it was something about this piano of Andy's that was different. Something mysterious. Bill, Roberta, Sandra, and Jan could also tell from the reaction of the others that it was more than just the most beautiful music they had ever heard. Ron was too concerned about Stefanie to think clearly and Andy was about to collapse. Finally Bill was able to break the spell by blurting out "Man Stefanie, I wish I had what you had tonight. Maybe I could sculpt something that would sell."

Julia jumped in with a very loud, "Bill!" and went over to help Ron with comforting Stefanie. In a few minutes they began to move around and soon all were standing next to or leaning against the piano. The congratulations to Stefanie were then made and accepted and she seemed to have recovered somewhat. Some wine was poured and it was decided that would be enough piano playing for the evening. The party returned to the living room and Jan found some small edibles to put out and the conversation returned to more normal topics.

Andy, Jason and Steve returned to the garage after a while. Each had the same thoughts. Andy knew something that he wasn't going to let be known so he remained silent. Steve looked a Jason and spoke first.

"There is something special about this piano. I don't know what it is or why it is, but it really is obvious.

Stefanie was as perfect as any pianist I have ever heard. Perfect."

He had been looking at Jason as he knew him much better than Andy, and Jason answered.

"You could tell that immediately. That was a world class performance. Those two pieces aren't the most difficult ones you could choose but they are not easy to play. That was astonishingly good."

There was a few seconds of silence and then Steve and Jason both turned to Andy and Jason asked. "Do you know something we don't?"

"No, not really." stammered Andy. "It's just a piano. I know it sounds great. At least I do know that now. What happened to Stefanie? Why was she crying?" Andy knew but he wasn't going to tell anyone, at least not yet. He was hoping his questions would sidetrack them from theirs.

Just then Jan stuck her head into the garage to tell Andy that Ron and Stefanie were leaving and wanted to say good evening. Andy jumped at the chance and left Jason and Steve to try to sort out their thoughts. He walked them to their car and Stefanie tried, unsuccessfully, to say good night and the tears came again. Andy took her hands, drew her close moving her away from Ron just a little and whispered.

"Stefanie, there is something magical about this piano. I can't tell you about it now. And maybe I never will. It will have to wait. I am not going to let any one else play it again until I can figure out what to do. Give me some time on this. Please."

Stefanie looked Andy in the eyes, trying to pull him closer with his hands still holding hers, and answered.

"I will try, Andy, but that was something I have never felt before while playing a piano. It was like falling helplessly in love. It was more than overwhelming. Wonderful. I wanted to keep on playing but suddenly, just as I was finishing *Rhapsody,* it was like I was told that is all the time you get. Andy, what just happened?"

Ron stepped in and wanted to know what was going on. Andy released his grip on her hands and Stefanie turned to him and said, "I was telling Andy I fell in love with his piano and at the end of *Rhapsody* the piano told me enough of you. I know it sounds crazy. I have never experienced anything like that before. I felt a moment of greatness and then it was gone."

CHAPTER 22

Andy's decision not to let any others play the piano was not particularly rational but he did have a motive. What had transpired with Stefanie a few nights ago made him sure she had made contact with whatever was going on with it. He was unsure whether the piano could just transfer it's magic to another at will or not. He knew most who had contact with it had no reaction. So far only Stefanie had seemed to and it was not what he had sensed but was more a gift to her as a pianist for a short time. He couldn't risk losing the magic. At least not yet.

After everyone had left after the playing he told Jan he was going to clean up the garage a little more and would cover the piano with the king sized bed sheet he picked up at Goodwill. He first went to the Case's curve and placed his hands on the rim. He let out a sigh of relief as the sensation came on fast and strong. Stronger than it ever had. He hadn't lost the magic and it seemed he had been given reassurance that it was still his to have even if some had been shared with Stefanie.

His desire to play was now starting to consume his every thought. The fact that for the first time in his sculpture career he had a work that was selling was of little importance to him. The gallery in Palm Desert had not only sold number 2 but now wanted number three for display and would buy it out right. Almost unheard of in the gallery business as they work on a very favorable consignment strategy taking forty percent commission on sales. His gallery in Breckenridge, on seeing the photos, requested number 4 as soon as possible. He asked Bill to ship number two and start the casting of the next three in the edition, three, four and five.

Andy had tried to sleep that night but shortly after midnight gave up and in his pajamas headed back into the garage. He pulled the sheet off and sat down on the chair in front of the keyboard. He had played with the keys a number of times pretending to play the first few notes and chords of *Rhapsody* and he positioned his hands over what he had chosen were the keys to press. He sat there motionless fearing what would happened if he touched them. Finally he took in a deep breath and did. He was spot on and in disbelief pressed them again with even more determination. Then again and once more. He sat back and thought, "Oh my God!" It was then the next few chords in sequence. He let the sounds of the last chord carry by stepping on the right pedal.

Jan had opened the door to the garage, sticking her head in, just as he hit the three cords in order and before she could stop herself said loudly, "What the hell are you . . . . What did you just do?"

Andy jumped up turning red with embarrassment and came up with, "Nothing."

"Oh no you don't Andrew Miller! You just started to play *Rhapsody in Blue*, didn't you?"

"Ah."

"Andy what is going on? Tell me! I have got to

89

know. Now! Do you hear me? Right now!" She pulled over one of the stools and sat facing Andy, who had sat back down as fast as he had jumped up, not with rage but inquiry written all over her face. Both in their pajamas, barefoot in the garage, sitting facing each other in front of one of the most beautiful piano's ever made.

Andy opened his mouth to speak but nothing came into his mind for him to say. He closed his mouth and then tried again. He got out. "Jan."

"Yes! . . . .Yes!Yes!"

"Jan, it is something like magic. Don't laugh. It's true. Every time I touch the piano I feel something magical. Stefanie felt it in another way last night. What made her cry was she had it while she played but just as she finished it disappeared. She described it like falling madly in love and then having that love taken away. She knows the piano is magical but I am certain she does not understand it."

"So now it's two of you who are crazy. No. No!" Jan sounded desperate and she was.

"Jan, please listen to me. When I first touched the piano at the foundry auction I felt something, a sensation like feeling, in my hands which then ran up my arms and into my chest. The light in the building dimmed and all the sounds of the auction faded out. I repeated the touching two more times with the same result. Even more intense each time. I had Bill come over and press his hand in the exact same place and he felt nothing. Do you want to see if you feel it?"

"Oh, God no. Andy, what is happening to you?" She stood up as if to leave as Andy blurted out. "I want to play this piano. I want to be good at playing it. Not another piano. Not any other piano. This piano. My piano."

Jan started to cry and Andy reached out to her and then held her tight trying to help her understand what was happening to him. Two middle aged adults, clinging to each other in their pajamas in the garage at half past two in the morning. Andy thinking he had told her as best he could and Jan thinking he may be slipping away from her. Both hoping it would be better when the sun came up. It was somewhat but this was when the real problems started because Andy was now determined to learn how to play his piano.

CHAPTER 23

Jan had headed off to her office feeling tired and confused. She couldn't decide whether she should talk to someone about last night's garage conference or not. Not seemed the better approach. She would see how things went in the next few days. Andy was her rock. He always seemed to find the way to carry on no matter what happened in their lives.

She hadn't known him when he had been laid off the first time from an engineering job in the San Francisco Bay area. He had spent the summer camping and working as a laborer in construction at Mammoth Lakes in the Sierras followed by the winter skiing in Aspen, Colorado. They met the following Fall when he had returned to the Bay area to rejoin a group of friends and to take a new engineering position.

His start in sculpture had began there and occurred because when she had seen a piece of metal wall sculpture she wanted for their new home he told her he could make one just like it. She called his bluff by enrolling him in an adult education class in metal sculpture. Then he went and made it. Another lay off and it was into the art world full time. A move to Aspen for a fun if not financial successful ten years was followed by a variety of experiments at making a living and then had them now settled in Loveland with Andy back in sculpture full time and her in a new career in real estate.

The entry of the piano into their lives was a complete surprise and she feared it's complication might cause another shakeup just as they seemed to be finally making progress financially. It had brought them together with a great group of new friends that she valued and it was already seeming to affect all of them to some degree. Even worse was the idea that the piano was actually having some control over the events. She simply couldn't accept that.

Andy had explained it to her as best he could and that seemed to worsen her apprehension. The idea that a piano could possibly control their lives was not in any way believable. She could only hope that what ever was happening would soon end.

He had agreed with Jan that he would have to spend more time on his sculpture as he had been neglecting it since he involved himself in the restoration. He agreed to a routine to devote equal time to each and not be consumed with the now newly identified piano project. His intentions were good and he made a start but it only lasted a few weeks. Or as Andy later would confess only a few days, or more accurately less than a day.

Andy headed to his studio early the day after he and Jan had come to the agreement on the piano project. Just as he reached his door Bill's studio door opened and out bounced Julia, the two them almost colliding. Andy turned to face her and say hello when he took a close look and found himself almost struck dumb by how pretty she really was. "Wow!" was his first words and then he manage to say, "Hi Julia, off to school?"

"Yep. Time to teach those young darlings some more music. I am really having fun and working with Stefanie is so great. She is really neat. See you later." And she was off down the stairs and out of sight before Andy could respond. He couldn't think of anything to say anyway. He thought that lucky bum Bill. She's smart, beautiful, and can sing.

He put his other thoughts about Julia out of his mind, or at least tried to, and entered his studio. He needed to start a new sculpture and just didn't want to start a new eagle piece which would be the smart thing to do. Andy knew that most sculptors, or painters, when they hit on something that sells they work up another similar piece to build on their customer base. He also knew it can be a trap as if you are too good at it you eventually start doing the same thing over and over. Andy didn't have that problem as he could go another month, or year, without detailing another feather.

He wandered about his studio somewhat aimlessly trying to think of what he should sculpt. His mind kept going back to the piano and how he was going to learn how to play it. His early experiment had been so successful he would continue along that line. Listen carefully to parts of the music, learning and then memorize what key, or keys, would produce that sound then repeat and repeat until he had it down.

He forced himself to consider starting a new sculpture. What came to mind first was to do a bust of a famous figure in music. Maybe Debussy. Debussy's *Clair de lune* was beautiful, relatively slowly played and didn't have a huge number of variables. This thought led him to maybe this should be his first piece to learn to play as a complete effort. Thinking this immediately made him realize he wasn't spending his studio time on his sculpture as he had promised Jan so he tried again. How about doing a bust of Debussy? People all over the world loved his music. Why wouldn't they appreciate his presence in their home with his likeness in bronze?

He was off to the library to do some research. Andy found Claude Debussy was a Frenchman, born August 22, 1862 and dying March 25, 1918 at age fifty-five years and unfortunately not very handsome. Creating his likeness might not result in a good sculpture. Maybe he should think this over. He checked out several books and would decide on Debussy later.

Art Myers

CHAPTER 24

Andy returned to his studio and put the books on the shelf, clearing and cleaning a spot first. It had been a nice walk to the library which was only three blocks away. He clicked on the little clock radio which was permanently tuned to NPR. It didn't make much difference to Andy what was being offered as it was mainly just background noise. But that wasn't going to work anymore.

He headed to his main supply store, Goodwill, and to the electronics section. As if preordained there sat a good looking Sony Receiver/Amplifier and matching five CD Disc Player at fifteen dollars each. Picking these up he headed to the bin of cables and picked up the cables he needed. Right next to the bin was a TKE headphones with a ten foot cable. He was set and it was off to pay for his treasures.

Andy had parked the van around the side of the Goodwill store as the front parking area was full. He was walking by the donation area and sticking up out of the trash dumpster were four furniture legs that looked like they must be attached to a small bench. One of the legs was at an odd angle but there was something there that had caught his eye. He went to his van and stowed the electronics and returned to the dumpster.

Andrew's Piano

Pushing aside some other useless items he pulled out the bench, grabbing the one leg that was falling off as he tugged on one of the good legs. Out of the dumpster he set it down on the pavement and held onto the freed leg. It was a piano bench. Not only a piano bench but an old one. The leather cushion was cracked and torn in a couple of places with some ugly looking stuffing pushing out. Andy looked around and spotted the old guy who was in charge of the donations area that day and called out, "You have any use for this?"

"Nah, it's just a piece of junk. Take it if you want it. One less thing to send to the dump."

Andy had a special little smile for situations like this and it spread on his face. It had only taken a glance to see the carving and workmanship that had gone into making this bench and the wood was in pretty good shape. The few seriously damaged areas he could easily fix. A new leather cushion would cost some but the end result would be in keeping with his piano. Another great day at Goodwill.

It was two trips up the stairs to his studio with his treasurers. He decided to see if the electronics worked first and more space was required on the storage shelves. A fleeting sense of guilt passed quickly as he set aside more sculpture supplies to make room. You need good music to do fine sculpture was his rational. He plugged in and turned on the units which lit up as they should and plugging in the headphones Andy could hear something indistinguishable. Putting them on he set the tuner to FM and the dial to NPR and there was some classical orchestral rendering in brilliant high fidelity. He had scored.

The headphones cable was just long enough for

him to reach the bench. He sat on the floor and began a close inspection of his other score. The woodwork of the bench surrounding the cushion was elaborately hand carved and other than a number of bumps and bruises was in very good condition. The legs would need some care but all could be repaired. It would require a new cushion but Andy knew he could do all the work except for it. When restored and painted it could be placed in front any piano with pride and would look even better in front of his.

Andy had just removed the headphones when Bill stuck his head in the door and asked him if he wanted to grab a quick bite at the Corner Restaurant.

"Thanks Bill, I'll just eat my P&J here. Got to get at my sculpture or Jan will throw me out."

"She ought to anyway. That doesn't look like any sculpture to me. It does look like a road kill piano bench. Don't tell me anything about it. I don't want know. See you later." He turned and was off down the stairs.

Andy remained seated on the floor looking around his studio. So far he hadn't made much progress towards his promise to Jan. He had no desire to start a new sculpture. He had no fear of not being able to do the work. He just lacked the desire.

Putting the headphones back on the one o'clock newscast was over and the next hour was going to be Rachmaninoff's *Piano Concerto No. 2*. He fixed and ate his P&J sandwich with a few potato chips and a diet Pepsi from the mini-fridge. He tasted none of it and when the two o'clock news break roused him from his concentration on the music he knew he was now in a tough spot.

Andy stood, stretched and then turned off the tuner. He took the library books off the shelf and sat on his wheeled stool and rolled over near the north side window and opened to the first page of the top book. It was a portrait of Debussy. At least the painter had improved his looks somewhat. Maybe he could do it too was as far as Andy could get at that moment. He sat there without turning another page for an hour.

CHAPTER 25

The next thing he clearly remembered was that he is in the garage sitting in front of his piano. It is uncovered but the Fallboard is down. Andy's first thought is "I am in trouble." Fortunately his recollection of the day slowly started to return. The walk to the library and the reference books on Debussy. The trip to Goodwill and setting up the electronics in his studio. The piano bench. The thought of the bench brings a smile to his face. "Maybe I am okay," he tells himself.

Andy positions the Fallboard and the beautiful Keyboard lifts his spirits. He runs his fingers gently over the ivory keys thrilling to their cool feel. His mind clears completely and he plays the opening chords of *Rhapsody* without a thought about what he is doing. He does it again and adds several more notes until he realizes that is all he has memorized.

He wonders how he could know what keys to play and what touch was required. He presses each key, from top to bottom of the scale and back again. They each seem familiar. Then he increases and decreases the force of the presses. Quick and then holding the key down. Then plays with the key touches and the pedals. This is something he needs to do to get the right sounds and tones. He will work at this whenever time and isolation are available. For right now he will not fight whatever has been given to him by the piano. Andy has no idea why this has happened but he won't question it.

He steps over to the CD player and punches the play button and Brubeck's Time Out comes on. Listening to *Take Five* carefully he then punches the number three track button, where it is located, and *Take Five* starts over. Twice more he does this, then turns the player off and sits down in front of the keyboard. Placing his hands over the keys he plays *Take Five* exactly as it was on the CD as played by Brubeck. He played it a second time. And then once more.

Andy sat very still, almost afraid to move. This is not a dream. He is able to play his piano by memorizing the sounds from the recording, translating them in his mind to sound of the particular keys on his piano. And then play those keys. It seems to him almost effortless. It hadn't been some kind of fluke that he was able to play those chords of *Rhapsody*. He could actually learn to play them by just memorizing the sounds.

Jan arrived home after an exhausting day. She had two showings, wrote a contract, and sat in on the long closing of one of her sales. A profitable day but it taken all her energy. She almost didn't want to see where Andy might be but went towards the door to the garage just as it opened. Andy looked equally haggard, almost sickly. They each stared at each other and when Andy said "Hi," with a weak grin Jan started to laugh and they embraced with one of their better hugs in some time.

At the same time they both asked each other, "How was your day?"

Art Myers

Jan was first to respond. "We've been married too long."

"No we haven't!" was Andy's response.

They decided to go to one of the small family restaurants they liked on Fourth Street for dinner and entered to find Jason and Roberta just being seated so they joined them. It had been just a few days since the first playing the piano by Stefanie in the garage. They caught up with chit chat which was a great relief for Andy as he really hadn't made much progress on either the piano or his sculpture. He certainly didn't want to talk about his just made promise to Jan on dividing his time.

Jan volunteered she had just had an exhausting day and that was the reason she and Andy were out for dinner. Andy reluctantly offered that he had found an old piano bench at Goodwill that needed restoring and could immediately feel Jan's stare penetrate his being. Luckily Roberta announced their travel plans to visit Steve and Sandra Pardee in Indiana for a week. They were going to drive and make it a no schedule road trip and be back in about two weeks.

"That sounds like fun for you both," Jan offered. "Stefanie called me the other day. She and Ron want to have the group over to their place soon. Shall I tell them about three weeks from now would be good?"

"That would be good for us." Roberta said as she looked at Jason for the expected nod of approval he was already giving to her.

Andy was now comfortable as the conversation had quickly left the piano bench. He added that Ron had told him he had just about finished the addition he was building on their house. "It is pretty major. A raised living

102

room on the west side so they get a panoramic view of the Rocky Mountains. Should be spectacular. He is a very talenmted guy. Did it all himself."

They left the restaurant in good spirits with hugs and a handshake.

Jan commented. "What nice people they are. So comfortable together and comfortable to be with." She then paused for a moment. "Now what is this about a piano bench that needs to be restored?"

CHAPTER 26

Andy managed to satisfy Jan with his explanations of the piano bench, the electronics purchase, and his trip to the library and thinking he might try to do a bust of Debussy. She was doubtful about the Debussy bust but decided not to make an issue of it as Andy might at least get his hands on some clay and start sculpting again. Anything he started would be better than not starting.

In the studio Andy found the headphones wouldn't work very well when sculpting. Their fidelity was perfect for his planned memorizing scheme but when moving about the cable would be a burden. It was off to Goodwill to pickup a pair of speakers. A nice pair were waiting for him and in thirty minutes he was listening to music in his studio without the use of the headphones.

He had just placed a modeling board on the sculpture stand when Bill came in. He looked worried and asked Andy if he had a few minutes.

"Sure. You know I always have a few minutes for a friend. What's up?"

They pulled up the stools and sat. Bill was a bit slow in getting started but Andy waited.

"Julia wants to get an apartment."

"So."

"Ah," was all Bill could manage.

"You don't mean by herself, do you?" Andy almost shouted.

"Oh no. For the two us. It's just that . . ." Bill was almost stuttering.

"You idiot. Do it. Do it today if you can. Don't let her get away!" Andy was now yelling. "She is the best thing that has ever happened to you!"

.   Bill sat there nodding his head in the affirmative. After about minute of head nodding he said, "Your right. I know that but I like my life right now. I don't want to sound stupid but it is cozy. Everything I want in the world is in one small space. Secure. I am afraid of changing it."

"Everything you have that is worth a damn is Julia. You can't expect her to be happy sleeping on a mattress on the floor and hanging her clothes on a bar on the wall forever. You can get along just fine without that cozy feeling you have right now as long as she is by your side. An apartment will be great and within a month you will think why didn't you do this sooner."

"Your right. Your right." A long pause was followed by, "Do you think Jan could help us find a place."

"She would love to. Especially to help Julia. She loves her."

Bill got up and looked down at Andy still seated. "I needed to hear that. You are a best friend, Andy. People need best friends." He retreated to his studio and closed the door.

Andy just sat there for a while thinking about what had just happened. Bill was right, people need good friends. He may be needing some of the ones he had now if things get out of hand in what he was planning.

But first was this Debussy bust. He built up the armature using pieces of two inch blue foam board, hot gluing them together on the armature post and cutting away unwanted areas with a serrated knife. Soon he had the basic head shaped with blocks below for the abbreviated shoulders. He had turned on his clay heater when he first came in this morning and the clay would have softened up by now.

Before grabbing the first handful of clay he turned on the CD player and hit the number one CD and *Clair de lune* filled the studio. He punched the Repeat button and then started applying the first layers of clay quickly and had the basic bulk that defined a typical bust portrait done in less than an hour. Examining the head position on the painting and those of the photos he had chosen he tweaked the head tilting it back and to the left a little. Satisfied with this he firmed up the clay a bit and decided it was time to let his work set and the clay harden before getting into more detail.

After cleaning his hands of clay he chose to sit and read a little more about Debussy. Donning the headphones he was hearing *Clair de lune* for the third time. It was being played by an Asian female pianist. A very good pianist, he thought.

From the library books Andy learned that Debussy had lead quite a life during his fifty-five years. Multiple affairs, mistresses, wives and having a single daughter late in his life who seemed the only person he was able to stay devoted to. His life was dominated by chance. He was the eldest of five children to parents of very modest means. In 1870, at seven years old, his mother then pregnant fled Paris with him and a sister to Cannes during a revolution on which his father had chosen the wrong side. There he was offered piano lessons paid for by an Aunt. Returning to Paris a year later the mother of a friend of his father's, who was his prison-mate at the time, continued the lessons. At ten he was accepted into the Conservatoire de Paris where he spent the next eleven years. *Clair de lune* was part of his Suite Bergamasque composed in 1890 but not published until 1905. It's inspiration is thought to have been from a poem of that name by Paul Verlaine written in 1869. It is the third movement of the Suite.

One of Andy's favorite sayings is in respect to life's opportunities "You have to be in the right place, at the right time, and have the right stuff." Certainly Debussy fulfilled that postulate.

CHAPTER 27

Andy entered his studio a little earlier than usual. He went straight to the Debussy sculpture. He was pleased to see what he had done yesterday was looking pretty good. He usually worked very slowly, making many small alterations trying to get it just right. This time he had worked almost not thinking and the results pleased him. He then started thinking, "Maybe I can do this. Combine my memorization of the music with sculpting."

He pulled the sculpture stand closer to the storage shelves. Turned on the clay heater and positioned his references, the painting of the young Debussy he liked and a page of photos of him in the other of the two of the books he had from the library. He would be careful not to get any clay on the pages as he would using proportional calipers to make guidelines on the head.

Turning on the CD player and putting on the headphones he punched the Play button and *Clair de lune* was back. He established the references from the photos. The first were easy as to the top of the forehead to the eyes, eyes to the bottom of the nose, eyes to the mouth and mouth to the chin. The widths of the eyes, nose and mouth were marked. He established the lines for the front of the ears, their height and width and position relative to the line through the eyes. All these were marks made in the clay with a small metal tool with a round point.

Stepping back he was surprised by how accurate they seemed. Almost always something would be off far enough to be noticeable and once that happens everything else gets tangled up in the proportions.

Step one was to gouge out the eye sockets making them a little deeper than one would think necessary and rolling marble size balls for eyes and push them into place. Another appraisal and again it looked about right.

Maybe it was *Clair de lune*, or Debussy himself, but this was going along quite nicely. Andy thought he better not go to far with that line of thinking. He had enough going on in his head already. He sensed someone was near, turned around removing the headphones.

Julia stood there looking just as she should with a nice smile but a slight watering of her eyes.

"Thank you Andy. Bill told me what you did for me. I mean us. It's going to work out fine. I will make it work. Jan will help us too. You two are special." She turned and was off down the stairs before Andy could respond. He felt a little embarrassed but also good to have apparently said the right things to Bill. They too were special.

A little later there was the sound of a bouncing basketball outside. Several times a week, at about a normal break time, a game of Horse took place at the parking lot of the church that faced Fourth Street just across the ally from the studio. Andy looking down saw about six people there starting to take shots at the backboard ring that stood on the east side property line. He hadn't participated since the piano had come into his life and he could use break right at this moment.

Andy was greeted as a long lost member and welcomed back. The ball was tossed his way and he made a one hand shot from well behind the free throw distance and watched the ball go though the hoop touching only net. It was the only shot made of his five attempts.

Back with Debussy, both recorded and sculpted, Andy spent until early afternoon concentrating on both. Things were going good. He thought he had about a third of *Clair de lune* memorized, the easier third, and was a long way in getting the bust near the detailing point. He never worked this fast. He was actually enjoying what he was doing. He didn't even feel guilty about the piano at that moment.

Just as he was ready to close up the studio Jan came up the stairs. "Hi big fella. Quitting already?"

Andy was surprised but could tell from her voice that she was happy about something. "Hi good looking. Come on into my studio. What's your name again?"

"Just call me Jan for now," and she swept past him into the studio. She first saw the bust of Debussy and kept up the banter. "Now who might that be. Not very handsome. Maybe you can help him out a little."

"Meet my good friend Claude Debussy. Claude this is Jan from down the street. You keep your hands off her. Oh that's right, you don't have any hands. Good." Andy was pleased that they were having a good exchange. Jan then took a closer look at the sculpture and walked all the way around it.

"Andy, that's pretty good. I don't know why, but I like what you have done so far. You started it only yesterday didn't you?"

Andrew's Piano

Now Andy knew something was different and Jan explained. "I am meeting Julia and Bill in a few minutes to show Dennis White's little house just across the street and down one block. It was just listed as a rental and I think it will be perfect for them. We met Dennis about 6 months ago. Remember? He is an architect and does a little sculpting. He just finished renovating it and they would be the first tenets."

An hour later the lease was signed. Bill and Julia were excited and happy, Jan was thrilled to have helped them, and Andy was relieved that Jan hadn't even seen the piano bench in parts on the floor in the corner of the studio.

It was decided that the four of them deserved margaritas at Adelita's. Jan's treat.

CHAPTER 28

For the next two days Andy was in his studio for long hours. Headphones on listening to repeated playing of the CD of *Clair de lune* and working hard on the bust of Debussy. Both the memorizing and the sculpting were progressing at a fast pace.

The detailing of the sculpture had been more than successful. Each step seemed to be done correctly and by the end of the fourth day sculpting the bust was essentially finished. Even the hair, both head and beard, was laid on and shaped with amazing ease. The check bones were just right, the ears and nose almost perfect, and most importantly the eyes came out special. Andy couldn't believe he could have produced a piece this good in such a short time.

He was also very tired in a good sense. He liked what he sculpted and his head was now filled with *Clair de lune*. He was getting ready to leave for home and anxious about what would happen when he sat down in front of his piano when Bill came waltzing in. "Man, you have been busy at this all week. Your working so hard you're no fun being around anymore."

"Come on Bill, it's only been four days. It's about time I put some effort into my sculpture."

Bill let out a laugh. "I looked in on you several times and you've got those headphones on and look like you are on another planet. Have to admit you were working pretty hard on Mr. Debussy there. Let me take a look at him."

Bill walked around the sculpture, then looked closer and then closer yet. He then stepped back and slowly moved left and right as he faced it. "How did you do that?"

"What do you mean, how did I do what?" Andy questioned as he was unclear of what Bill was asking.

"You haven't seen it yet?"

"What? Come on Bill, what the heck are you talking about?"

"Debussy is staring right at you and his eyes follow you around. Come here and walk back and forth in front of that guy. He is looking at you."

Andy did and sure enough for most of the angle looking at the full face the eyes seemed to follow you. Sometimes that happens in a painting but not very often in a sculpture. Debussy was looking at Andy, following him as he moved about. It was very disconcerting and even worse he seemed to have a twinkle in his eyes.

"That's a piece of work, Andy. A good one. Wonder what Jan will say when he stares at her? Gotta go. Julia will be home in a few minutes and we are planning our move. Don't have much to move. It's going to work out. Thanks."

Bill was out the door and Andy was still caught in the gaze of his own making.

Andy decided to turn Debussy around to face out one of the studio windows. He could stare at what ever was going on outside. Andy sat down on one of the stools and gave all this a little more thought. He was hoping when got home he would have enough time before Jan arrived to see if he had *Clair de lune* down. But it was the sculpture he was really thinking about. It had actually come out pretty good and he liked what he had done. Usually he would find some little fault in a work and that would become a focal point for him. It would be there, often in the casting, and he would see it first whenever he looked at the piece. He hadn't detected one in this work and the eyes were so good it scared him a little. Especially when they followed you about.

Andy decided he would do a bust of every composer whose music he would try to play. Gershwin would be next as *Rhapsody in Blue* was on the list. He would see if this concentration on the music would translate to his sculpting. Wouldn't that be a kick if the piano had brought a new skill to his sculpture.

Andy had plenty of clay. Busts didn't require very much. One of the first people he met in Loveland had a photo studio in George Patterson's main building and as a part time money maker would produce Loveland Clay. It was a messy combination mixing Georgia Kaelin clay, melted beeswax, and an evil Vaseline like petroleum substance. In trade for Andy's labor he ended up with three hundred pounds. Enough for life size sculpting. About ten hours of hard labor in a dark, dirt floored, unfinished concrete block building the two of them made nearly three thousand pounds of the stuff.

He now had a plan that might work with his agreement with Jan. He could sculpt the busts of the composers while he memorized their music. Maybe both sides of this equation would balance.

Andy went over to the Debussy bust and asked "Do you like the view from here? Okay, I will leave you right there." Great, he thought, "I am now talking to a sculpture."

CHAPTER 29

Andy got home about three and Jan had left a note that she had showings and wouldn't be home until six. It was time he tried the playing of the entire *Clair de lune* and see if his memorizing and sculpting effort would work. The sculpture of Debussy exceeded his expectations and it was now time to test the piano playing. A quick washing of his hands and he was in the garage removing the sheet from the piano. It seemed to have a special radiance right then that made him smile. He folded the Front Top Board back and lifted the Boards up and positioned the Prop. As it happened each time he looked down into the interior he marveled at the beauty and ingenuity that was displayed. One of man's great achievements was always his first thought.

He moved the chair into position and remembered that he had made no progress on the restoration of the bench. Tomorrow he would set aside some time to start on that but right now he had another kind of work to do. The Fallboard was lifted and pushed back and the Keyboard had it's turn to dazzle him. Putting both hands on the Music Shelf he waited until the sensation he expected came and then positioned his hands to play the first soft notes of *Moonlight*. He played them just right and he easily progressed through the entire piece as if he had been playing it for years. At little over four and a half minutes to complete he couldn't contain his satisfaction and played it again. As the last notes were played his eyes started to tear up. "Debussy, how were you able compose something this good. This beautiful."

Andy sat there for almost an hour. He was happy. What an unusual feeling it was. A moment when everything in your consciousness seems just right. A true balance. He had this feeling a few times before but it had been a while and never had it been this strong. He didn't want to move. He was doing exactly what he wanted to do, how he wanted to do it, and he had been able to do it.

Then a thought slowly entered his mind. "How can I share this with Jan? Is now the time or will it all disappear if I share it? What will I do if it suddenly leaves me like it left Stefanie after her playing the piano a few weeks ago?" Andy mulled this over and was still in a ponder when the garage door started rising.

"Ah, the maestro is at work I see," Jan remarked as she exited her car in the driveway and walked into the garage. "Why do you look so sad my best friend?"

Andy gave her a smile and replied, "I just like to sit here and look at the piano. Isn't she a beautiful lady?"

"So now it's a lady. You need to name her then. But first get the groceries out of the trunk. My showings went faster than I expected so I stopped and did some shopping. There is a rib-eye steak in there. Interested?" Jan asked as she disappeared into the house. Andy would share Debussy with her later.

After dinner, medium rare and pan fried to perfection, Jan suggested they take a walk. Andy said "Let's go to Benson Park and stroll among the sculptures."

They closed up the town home and drove the short distance to the Park. It was just past the north end of Lake Loveland, less than a half mile, but walking in the Park was so much better than along the very busy Taft Avenue. The Benson Park Sculpture Garden was becoming one of the best sculpture gardens in the United States, even rivaling Brookgreen Gardens in South Carolina. It was a perfect evening and the enjoyment of being surrounded by so many fine works was increased by personally knowing so many of the sculptors. Andy and Jan held hands as they walked slowly along the paths that surround the fine collection of sculptures.

"Will you get one of yours selected?' Jan asked.

"Maybe some day. Remember last August I managed to get a last minute invite into the Sculpture in the Park show with three of my earlier works. It is going to be harder to get invited as more and more sculptors want in. They select the works for the park through the show and if your not participating you don't have much of a chance."

"Well you better get busy and do some pieces that demand their attention," was Jan's reply. Andy's thought was a bust of Debussy wouldn't be high on their list but he didn't share this with her. "Maybe someday," he added.

After they returned home there was a call message from Stefanie and Jan returned it. The planning for the party at the Stevens's was underway. This was something that Andy didn't have to be involved in. He went into the garage and played through *Clair de lune* one more time and then said good night to his piano and covered her up.

"Did you have your stereo on in the garage? I thought I heard *Clair de lune*. Sounded really good to me.

Who was playing it?"

Andy shrugged, smiled at Jan, and answered by asking about the plans for the party. She may of told him but his mind was elsewhere, as it seemed to be more and more often.

CHAPTER 30

Andy was back to his studio early again and noticed Bill's door was open. It was the first time he had seen it open since Julia had arrived. He knocked just in case and Bill yelled "Come on in whoever you are." Which he did.

Bill was seated in front of one of his sculpture stands busy at work. Andy came closer and looked at what he was working on. It was now his turn to ask, "What is that?"

"What do think it is?"

"It looks like five plump little birdies sitting on a wispy little tree branch. Damn but their cute. Where did this come from?"

Bill turned to face Andy with a big grin on his face. "Julia said to me a while ago that I should lighten up and just do something without thinking about it. Forget whether it would sell or what anyone might think. Just let go and do it." He then pointed to his storage shelf and Andy saw four or five different variations of these little birds in bronze mounted in haphazard poses on posts, rocks, and branches. Some were in threes, some in sevens, and one neat little single. There were also several little rabbit bronzes in whimsical orientations, even a sly fox.

Andrew's Piano

Andy was dumbfounded. "Where did all this come from. Your other work was pretty good but nothing like this."

"You told me that Julia was the best thing that ever came into my life. I knew that the first day I met her. Then she got me started in this line and now they just come about with hardly any effort on my part. The galleries love them because they have such a good price point. They fit into discretionary spending. The wife visiting the gallery while her hubby is out on the golf course going through a couple of hundred dollars can buy one of these for about that much and doesn't even have to ask if it is okay."

Andy didn't exactly know what to say. They were neat sculptures. Not only fun pieces but with the design and really innovative patina were in truth fine sculpture. "Bill, those are really neat sculptures. They work. How the production going?"

"That's the beauty of these. I am using the Casting Shop in Berthoud to do full service. Even the shipping. I just give them the name, address and the sculpture's ID. Julia is handling the book work."

"You've got something really good here. You know that. Run with it. My only advice is once in a while take on a bigger, more challenging project and do it just for yourself. Don't even have it cast if it doesn't work. You understand what I'm getting at, don't you?"

Bill looked at Andy. "Sure I do. I already have a few ideas wandering around in my head and when the time is right I will start one. I won't get trapped by this."

Andy gave Bill a firm pat on the back and headed back to his studio.

He had two reference books on George Gershwin

from the library and he loaded three different CD's with *Rhapsody in Blue* in the player and hit the play button. Two were orchestra concerts with piano and the third was a solo piece by an American pianist. With the headphones on he started to read about George.

His parents had left Russia as young people, first his mother with her family and later his father following his true love as soon as he could afford to get to New York City. George was the second son, Ira was the first, and was born in September 1898. A third boy, Arthur was born and then the youngest sibling, a girl, Francis. They grew up in the Jewish tenements near the Yiddish Theater District and had a normal childhood for the time and place until a piano entered their home when George was around ten. It was George that took to it rather than Ira, although all four showed musical talent early and into their futures.

One of George's piano teachers had encouraged him to attend orchestral concerts. Following such concerts he would try to play, on the piano, the music he had just heard from recall. Andy was of course struck by this. George Gershwin would try to play music he had heard in a concert by hearing the notes and then playing the keys that would produce them. He sat there holding the book and he read this a second time. He surmised that maybe he wasn't as crazy as it seemed. But on the other hand that was George Gershwin and he was Andy Miller.

Early in 1937 at the very peak of Gershwin's productivity, most of which can be immediately recognized as George Gershwin like *Rhapsody in Blue,* he began having severe headaches and started losing dexterity. He died July 11, 1937 at the age of thirty-eight from a brain tumor.

How unfair thought Andy. Andy's father had died

of a brain aneurysm at fifty-six. He had always thought that that had been so unfair but thirty-eight was much too young. Especially for someone who had so much to offer. Nature's God can be cruel.

"Enough of this for now," thought Andy. It is time for George Gershwin.

CHAPTER 31

After three days of concentrated studio time Andy was getting close to finishing his sculpture of Gershwin and had spent hours of time listening to *Rhapsody in Blue*. He had found a piano solo by a Latvian pianist he liked even better than the American one he had planned to use. *Rhapsody* was more complicated than *Clair de lune* and ran almost fourteen minutes versus four and one half minutes for *Clair*. It was going to be a real test for him.

Around four in the afternoon Bill was getting ready to head home, one block away, when he noticed Andy's door was still open. He called out in a low voice. "Andy, are you in there?" There was no response so he stepped inside to find him sitting on his work stool, headphones on, starring blankly at the bust of George Gershwin that he had been working on. Bill could see the decibel meters on the stereo were at zero so he knew Andy wasn't listening to anything. Concerned, he walked over and put his hand on his shoulder. "Andy, are you okay?"

Andy turned to look at whoever had just touched him and immediately recognized Bill. "Hi Bill, what's up? I must have been lost in some big thought. Didn't hear you come in." He pulled off the headphones and sheepishly added, "Can't hear anything with these on."

Andrew's Piano

Bill could tell that something wasn't just right but he decided not to press the issue. "George is looking pretty good there. He sure has a long narrow face and that's some chin. It is a good likeness. I think you can put him over there next Claude. Hope they get along with each other." Andy smiled and looked at his sculpture and a puzzled look came over his face.

"You better be getting home pretty soon, the party at the Stevens's starts in an hour and Jan will be upset if you are late. . . . Andy are you okay?" Bill asked for the second time knowing Andy could hear him this time.

"Yeah, I'm fine. Must have dosed off for a few minutes. I'll close up here and see you at Ron and Stefanie's in an hour."

Bill headed out still concerned but Andy seemed himself even if briefly looking a bit befuddled. He didn't like to see his friend in other than fine spirits and full of enthusiasm.

Andy sat still trying to remember the day. This had happened to him just a couple of weeks ago when he found himself sitting in front of his piano in the garage and didn't remember how he got there. That time the memory came back quickly and he hoped it would again this time. He looked at the Gershwin bust and could see it was finished. He couldn't remember finishing it. It looked damn good, he thought.

A seed of worry started to germinate and he hoped there wasn't something bad going on in his brain. Also was where had he gotten to in memorizing *Rhapsody*. He thought he had it pretty much done and then it dawned on him that the last thing he could clearly remember was thinking, "I am ready."

Andy quickly closed up the studio and George was now right next to Claude, looking out the window. Jan greeted him as he walked in the door with hurry up instructions. He showered, shaved a second time for the day, and put on the clean cloths Jan had set out for him. In the rush to get ready he put aside thinking about what had happened in the studio that afternoon.

On the fifteen minute drive out to the Stevens's Jan could tell that there was something bothering Andy. She reached out and put her hand on his thigh, gave it a squeeze, and tried the usual "How was your day?"

"Good. The Gershwin bust is done and looks nice. I think I caught his likeness pretty good. Sort of a funny looking man in a way. Narrow face, high forehead, distinctive nose, and big chin. Even his eyes are proportionately a tad small. I used the best photo I could find that I liked. It was taken in 1936, the year before he died. He had an expression that caught my eye. Something like he may have know that all was not just right in his life but that he was okay with that. That is an odd reason for me to use it, but I liked it and I like what I did."

Jan thought that was a odd reason, too. But if Andy was happy with the bust she was comfortable with his reasoning. She had no idea how he would be able to market these pieces but he was actively sculpting again and seemed more satisfied with his accomplishments with these two sculptures than any of the more recent ones he had done. The big eagle was selling and was a good piece but he seemed to merely take it for granted.

"Is anything just not right in your life right now?" Jan questioned.

"I don't think so. I think things are just fine in my

life right now," Andy answered, trying to sound convincing.

They swung into the Stevens's driveway next to two other cars that were parked there.

CHAPTER 32

Getting out of the car in the Stevens's driveway there was no doubt Ron had designed and built a very special addition onto to their house. It stretched twenty-four feet centered on the living room portion of the original house with the roof line angles proportioned to the main roof lines. Almost the entire face side was in glass facing west towards the Rocky Mountains. There was a large rock outcropping at the south side corner and the foundation was formed partially on and around it. The rest of the foundation was faced in matching rock. It's look was that it always had been part of the architecture.

Andy and Jan joined the rest of the group admiring Ron's design and workmanship. Inside the quality continued as the new addition was two steps up from the main floor and the new room's depth added fourteen feet. The kitchen had been increased in size and the original dinning area opened up making a functional great room with the magnificent stage like addition. New carpeting in the great room complimented the hardwood floors of the addition. Two big sectional couches and several large chairs made it a place to enjoy what Colorado was famous for and at that moment Mother Nature was doing her best to show it off.

Andy shook Ron's hand and he accepted the fourth

or fifth congratulation. Andy and Bill had come over and helped him place the big beams when the framing was up, but other than that, the foundation pouring, and the glass installation he had done all the work himself. It had come out spectacular.

The drinks were served and the conversation rolled along. Jason and Roberta's car trip to Indiana had gone great. They had visited the wild west sights, stayed one night on the Mississippi River, had a good visit with the Pardees, who sent their best to all, and had a nice drive back. Bill and Julia couldn't tell all how much they liked their new rental house and how happy they were. Andy and Jan were busy between the other six conversing on a variety of subjects. Ron and Stefanie were the proudest home owners in Loveland.

Just before dinner was to be announced Ron came over to Andy and said, "Andy, I have a room I want to show you. Since you were an engineer you might find it interesting." Just off the living room there was a door that lead to what was probably an office or storeroom. There were no windows but it was large, maybe fourteen by sixteen feet. When Ron clicked on the lights Andy was presented with a wall of rack mounted electronics, several consoles of more equipment, television screens, tape recorders, a large work bench and a big red ten drawer tool chest.

"Wow, were am I? In a NASA dream room preparing to equip the space station. What is all this stuff?" was the best Andy could do.

"It all started when I first went to work for Hewlett Packard. They have a surplus station where any equipment or parts deemed no longer needed are placed. Any employee who wants, or can use them, may take them. The only requirement is that they cannot be sold. This ranges from chairs, stools, work benches to some of the latest high technology equipment that is considered not functional, broken or damaged."

"Let me guess, you occasionally stopped by for a peek," Andy responded with a little tinge of envy in his voice.

"Occasionally, you might say." Ron walked over to a large, but portable, reel to reel tape recorder with half inch tape on ten and one half reels. Stacked directly behind it was a box of twenty matching reels.

"Are the reels loaded with tape?"

"Yes"

"Does the tape recorder work?" Andy continued.

"You bet it does. Perfectly."

"In other words you can record high fidelity sound."

Ron new where Andy was going with this and guided him back towards the group saying in a soft whisper, "I have a complete sound studio in there and behind the walls of the new room is wiring that can hook up everything I need to record, produce, mix, and make CDs. Stefanie doesn't know the whole story about my man cave and for now I want to keep it that way. You understand, don't you?"

"Completely," Andy assured him.

Dinner was served and the eight friends sat in comfort in the new room that Ron had built eating and watching the sun disappear behind the Rocky Mountains.

CHAPTER 33

As Andy and Jan headed home after the party at the Stevens Jan started a discussion on how great the new room is and how well the house functions. "It is such a good addition. He has added fifty percent to the value of their property."

"You sound just like a real estate salesman."

"You're right." Jan was quiet for a few seconds, then asked, "You know what that room needs, don't you?"

"Yes!"

They didn't say much more until they got home. Jan took Andy's hand and squeezed it tight." You are my all knowing wizard, aren't you?"

"Yes!"

The next morning at breakfast Andy told Jan he planned to take the day off. Maybe go hit a few golf balls, maybe even play nine. He needed a break and be outside some. She agreed and wished him a good day as she headed to her office. Andy knew that without her income he would probably have to give up sculpturing and find another job in engineering. His technical knowledge was out dated but he might be able to get another job in packaging design or parts procurement as he had just done in Illinois. Neither of those appealed to him. She seemed to be happy right now but his piano was becoming a cloud over her head and he knew it may get darker soon.

He headed for the garage. Removing the sheet he lifted the Boards and pulled the Prop into place. Sitting down in the chair he lifted the Fallboard and pushed it into place. Stretching out his arms he placed hands on the piano and felt the response. This would be his stiffest test yet. *Rhapsody in Blue* is a difficult thing to play. Even very good pianist can't handle some of its nuances and Andy could tell some of what he had memorized was not as clear as with *Clair de lune*. He had been able to play the first opening chords, his large hands and long fingers aiding in the reach required.

He took a deep breath and started to play. He got through the first few minutes and then the quick changes in rhythm started to confuse him a bit and he suddenly lost his place and got really off track so he stopped and started over. This time was a little better but again the fast fingering that seemed so natural to the ear was harder to do than he expected. Again he had to stop and start over. He now had another problem he hadn't figured on. He couldn't pick his place to make a correction. His memory was all start to finish. If he stopped he would have to start over at the beginning if he wanted to continue.

Andy sat back and pondered this new difficulty. He would either have to play it over and over until the end was practiced enough to be confident in playing it as he was with the beginning. The whole piece running at about fifteen minutes, this would take a really long time.

He started again and for the first three minutes it was now starting to become rote and sounded right to him. He found another secret that if he stopped and immediately practiced just the part that had tripped him up he could correct it and be ready the next time he got to that point.

Two hours later he had made it half way through Rhapsody but his hands and fingers were tiring and beginning to hurt. It was time to stop for the day. He closed up the piano and left the garage. He had no sooner turned on the television and stretched out on the couch than Jan walked in.

"Hi big guy. Looks like you got a lot done. How was golf?"

Andy gave her his best smile then told her he was going after lunch and was just waiting around for someone to fix him a sandwich.

"Fix your own. I have a showing in twenty minutes." Jan grabbed a few crackers, cheese and a soft drink and was out the door.

"What a woman," thought Andy.

Golf that afternoon didn't go much better than *Rhapsody* had. He decided to play only nine on the Olde Course in Loveland, less than a mile from the town home, and found no play and no practice in months left his poor game in terrible shape. He was paired up with a couple of good old boys of about his ability and other than the one par he scored on the fifth hole they all played to about the same dismal score. At least he got a little fresh air and exercise.

When he arrived back home Jan was there and was complaining about having shown some lookers, not buyers, and felt she had wasted her afternoon. "That's real estate!" she said.

Andy said, "That's golf!"

Life almost seemed normal but Andy knew *Rhap-*

sody was out in the garage waiting for another grueling session and he hoped he hadn't met his match. Also, his memory of finishing Gershwin had not come back.

CHAPTER 34

Andy spent the morning in the studio. He examined both the Debussy and Gershwin busts and came to the conclusion they were finished. He was still worrying about not being able to remember doing the finishing touches on Gershwin. The last he could remember was getting all the shapes and positions right and thinking it was time to do the detailing. Even working fast the detailing would have taken several hours at minimum. He remembered none of it.

Bill's door was closed so there was no opportunity to sit and talk. He didn't really think he had anything he wanted to talk about but not being able too didn't help his mood. The feeling of losing control of his life was starting to creep into his psyche and he didn't like it.

He rethought his plans. He now knew he could play the piano from memorization of others playing. *Clair de lune* he could play at will. He was confident of that. *Rhapsody* was being much harder for him and he may need some help getting through it. Since he had planned to keep this effort secret he was unsure whom to ask. Jason or Stefanie were the only choices available.

Since the big plan was to play five different popular works that he really liked and, once mastered, do some kind of concert. That would be to prove that all this would have been worth the time and effort he had spent on it. Beyond this he had no plan. Originally he was thinking of the value of the piano itself but that was no longer an option. He could never sell it. Then to do performances but that probably would not work just because of his nature and life style. He was sure the only piano he could play was this one. It was no clarinet that could be carried in a suitcase to a venue. His talk with Ron, and seeing his recording equipment the night before last, had him thinking of doing CDs to gain some financial return. Maybe that would work.

He sat down on a stool and rolled over between the two sculptures, looking first at Debussy, then at Gershwin. "What do you two guys think I should do?" He didn't expect an answer from either of them and much to his relief he didn't get one. He pushed his stool back and went through the CDs he had picked out. *Rhapsody,* played by the Latvian, was in the player's number one slot and *Clair de lune* by the Asia lady was in number two. He had placed the Earroll Garner's "Concert by the Sea" CD in three, Dave Brubeck's "Time Out" in four, and the *Rachmaninoff Piano Concerto No. 2 -Solo Piano* he had found in five.

Andy hit the play button and *Rhapsody* came from the speakers. He didn't want to hear it right then and selected three. That was the right choice. Sitting on his stool he let his mind just listen to Garner play the notes. He had no other thoughts. When it ended he stood up, turned off the system, closed the studio and headed back home and to the garage.

He set up the piano and positioned himself to play.

He was going to try to get farther into *Rhapsody* and put his hands on the piano and as the sensation started up his arms he brought them down and ran through the first parts without missing a note, almost getting through the part of extremely fast fingering correctly and enough to continue. Then he stumbled at the exact same spot he had the last two times. He couldn't reach the keys he needed. He needed help.

Andy decided to call Jason first as he knew that he would have to let whoever helped him know about the piano's magic. At least the magic it had for him and he wanted that kept secret. Also he may need a lot of time to get this sorted out and that might not work out very well with Stefanie for a variety of reasons.

Jason said he would be over in ten minutes. He broke his old record and was there in eight minutes. Andy led him into the garage and had him seated on a stool next to the piano. Jason was looking at it with a loving gaze he couldn't hide. "It is just beautiful Andy. Just beautiful."

"It most certainly is that, Jason. It is more than that and that is what I want to talk to you about." Andy paused. A long pause. Jason knew something important was about to happen that he was going to be privy to so he remained silent. "Jason, I am going to tell you something that I want, no need, you to keep a secret. Just between us. Can you do that for me?"

Now it was Jason's turn to remain silent for a moment. Then he responded, "What is it Andy? I will keep anything you tell me between us until you tell me it can be shared. Even to the grave."

Andy stood up and asked Jason to come with him to the curved side of the Case. "Place your hand right there," showing him the area that sent the sensations into his body. Jason did as requested and then looked at Andy.

"Do you feel anything unusual? Anything at all?" Andy asked.

Jason's face showed he was wondering what this was all about but also knew Andy was very serious about it, so he answered in the same manner.

"No. Nothing other than the delight of touching this magnificent piano. Should it have been more?"

Andy went back to the chair and sat down. Placing his hands in position he then proceeded to play *Rhapsody* through to the part he was having trouble with, first the fast fingering but he managed to stumble through it, and then to the place he couldn't press the keys he needed.

Jason was dumbfounded. "How did you learn to do that? Jesus Andy, how did you learn to do that?"

"Will you help me?" was Andy's answer.

Jason looked like he was about to pass out. "Any way I can. This is magic." And then for the second time he pleaded. "Andy, let me be part of this. Please, I have to be part of what is happening with this piano."

CHAPTER 35

Jason and Andy remained seated in the garage, neither speaking for several minutes. Jason was wondering how Andy had been able get so far into *Rhapsody* at that high a level and Andy was trying to think how to explain what was going on without appearing to be crazy.

Finally it was Andy that broke the silence. "Jason, it is very difficult for me to tell you what is happening here. I haven't told anyone, not even Jan. I am afraid if I do tell someone it will all be over for me and I will lose my piano. I am more than afraid, I am scared."

At first Jason made no effort to respond. Not only he didn't know what to say, he had no idea what was going on. But he knew something was and it had to do with the piano. After a long pause he decided to take a different tack. "Andy at the first party you had, you know with the team as you called us, you had on your stereo player five discs with a nice variety of jazz and classical. You had the volume low so we could talk and we really didn't pay much attention to the background music. A nice combination. Then when Stefanie had that performance at the first playing with Debussy's *Clair de lune* and Gershwin's *Rhapsody in Blue* I knew something was happening that had to be more than coincidence. Both of those pieces

139

were part of your choices for the party." He paused for a moment and could see Andy was listening. "This has something to do with the piano, doesn't it?"

Andy nodded yes and closed his eyes. He knew that now was the time. He either had to tell Jason the entire story, or at least part of it, if he was ask for help in playing the more difficult music. He decided on the part of it to respond.

He looked directly at Jason and started. "There is something about this piano. I am not going to tell you what it is exactly, but only what it does for me. I still want you to hold this as a secret for now. Okay?" Jason nodded in the affirmative and Andy continued. "When I was about half way through the restoration I began to get this over- whelming desire to be able to play it. Not just chop sticks or little tidbits but real music, really good music. Then when Stefanie played two of my favorites, and played them at the highest level for a pianist, I haven't been able to think of doing anything else."

"After Stefanie's performance I essentially hid the piano. I'm sure you have noticed that. I spent hours press- ing every key. Soft, hard, gently, in chords, using the ped- als, trying out everything I could think of. Then I memo- rized the the first parts of *Rhapsody*, only the opening part and played it almost without thinking. It just happens. I memorized all of *Clair de lune* by listening to it over and over remembering every note, the timing, rhythm, volume and damping. I sit down right where I am now, put my hands up here and when I sense I am ready, I start play- ing. For whatever reason, I seem to be able to play the piece exactly as I have heard it on the recording. My hands and fingers do exactly what they are meant to do without any conscious thought. That is what makes no sense and it has to have something to do with this piano."

Jason was now completely at a loss for words. It made no sense to him either. As a fairly good pianist himself, remembering the hours and hours of practice, of drills, exercises, playing scales and learning to read music that anyone could sit down at a piano and play as Andy apparently could was beyond belief.

"It's not possible, is it Jason?"

Andy turned and placed his hands on the piano. Waited the few seconds he needed and then played *Clair de lune* through without a blemish.

Jason couldn't speak.

Finally Andy broke the silence. "Let's talk about *Rhapsody*.

This brought Jason back to reality. He took a deep breath, which he desperately needed, and ventured, "Yes, lets talk about *Rhapsody*.

Jason began with some history. That Gershwin was commissioned by Paul Whiteman to combine classical music with jazz in an orchestral and piano composition. It was premiered in February, 1924 by Whiteman and his band and with him playing the piano. Gershwin was just twenty-six years old and this was the real launching point of his career. The jazz aspect of this endeavor was that it could interpreted by the pianist to a degree but it was so good in its original form that it hasn't varied much over the years. The clarinet "glissando" that starts every orchestral performance was a prank by the lead clarinetist at a rehearsal and remains to this day a must for any performance.

It was then that Jason tried to enter into Andy's

world. "*Rhapsody* is very difficult to play. That you have gotten this far into it at the level you are trying to copy is beyond my comprehension. What has happened is the recording you are memorizing from is by a pianist of the highest skill level and one who is showing that skill off. It would be better to find another source to memorize. It will still be an admirable performance but you could eliminate some of the subtle tricks this one is putting in."

Andy took all this in but then asked "Why do I stumble at that one point?"

Jason chuckled. "You have to play those notes with your left hand crossing over your right hand while it is playing its notes.

CHAPTER 36

"I should have been able to have figured that out. When Stefanie played it I wasn't watching her hands. I don't know what I was watching. It was so good I was just listening. What else can you do when you hear something like that?"

Jason's reply was simple. "Nothing else."

"Excuse me a minute. I will be right back." Andy stepped into the house and shut the door.

Jason stood and started to circled the piano. He stopped in front of the keyboard. Genuine ivory keys in perfect condition. Every pianist's dream. Raising his eyes he looked down on the Frame, just above the Pin Block, and could see all the strings attached to the pins and threaded through the agraffes, the bass strings over the mid strings. He then moved around and slid his hand on the rim and stopped at the curve of the case. Looking down he could see portions of the Soundboard, the Bridge, all the strings and the beautiful gold colored Frame. It glowed, there were no other words to describe it.

"Beautiful. Just beautiful," he thought. Man could land and step on the moon. An astounding achievement. You can marvel at the photographs, go to the Space Center and touch the capsule, but to be in the presence of and touching this piano was better than that. For Jason, so much better than that. He wiped away a few tears and returned to the stool just as Andy came back with the faint sound of a flushing toilet in the background.

Andy took his position, hands placed on the piano and then started *Rhapsody* again. As he started the very fast fingering he slowed the tempo ever so slightly and breezed through it. He crossed his left hand over his right and played through the problem area as if he had done it many times. He then played into the finish. Two spots caused an instantaneous change so slight most would not have detected it.

When he had finished Jason was again speechless. He finally blurted out, "That can't be done. Andy you can't do that. How did you do that?"

Andy was smiling. Not a big grin, just a trace of a smile of accomplishment. He knew he had made several mistakes but he was able to cover them. Somehow his brain could compensate. This was a new discovery and it gave him confidence that he didn't have to reproduce every note exactly the way the recording played them.

Jason was still silent.

Andy realized he owed Jason the full explanation so he told him the whole story from the time he first touched the case at the foundry during the IRS auction until he had just return from using the bathroom and putting his hands on the piano. He repeated about the hours spent learning of the notes and the memorizing of the recordings. He even told Jason about how much better his sculpting was going as he listened to the music he intended to play.

144

Andrew's Piano

"I still can't believe any part of this. This simply can't be happening." Jason was almost disconsolate.

"You can see why I don't want you tell anyone about this. I am trusting you to not speak about it to anyone." Andy was worried but he was sure Jason would honor his promise. He then told him what he thought had happened to Stefanie that night she played for the team.

"You remember Stefanie's performance. When she ended it she was crying and Ron had to comfort her. We all went back into the house. You and I, with Steve Pardee, came back out to the garage for a bit. You and Steve were thinking there must be something special about the piano and I deflected that it just sounded really good."

"Yeah, I remember that clearly. It was some special night," Jason said almost in a whisper.

"Stefanie was mumbling to Ron that she had never played so well. Never. Later, as they were leaving she told me it was like magic. She could play with no worry of hand and finger position. It was just the music she needed to play. It was like love at first sight. You don't have to think, just live it. And then just as she finished *Rhapsody* the feeling was gone. Disappeared in an instant."

"What you are telling me Andy is that you have that sense that you don't have to worry about anything as you play except the music and every thing else just happens with no thought on your part. You don't even think which keys you need to press, or even how you must press them. That's beyond me. It can't happen. It takes so much effort to play at this level. It's not possible."

"Jason, that is why I want your solemn promise not to tell anyone about this. Maybe someday, but not now. Not yet"

145

"You have my word, Andy. I will not mention anything of what you just told me. No one would believe me anyway."

CHAPTER 37

Andy was back in his studio the day after his meeting with Jason. He was a little concerned that maybe he shouldn't have told him the full story but he was relieved that somebody else knew about what was going on. Jason would understand if things went wrong in this quest of his and help Jan understand if he wasn't able to for any reason. It wasn't a rational thought that something would go wrong but it lingered in his mind that he was stretching the boundaries lines a bit.

Today he was going to decide the next piece, or pieces, he would memorize and then play. His choices were Rachmaninoff, Brubeck, and Garner. Rachmaninoff's *Piano Concerto No.2 - Solo Piano* was a difficult one and he needed a little break after *Rhapsody* He also wanted to sculpt a bust that had more character. He decided on Erroll Garner. In addition to his recognizable playing style he had a great face. Also, Garner's "Concert by the Sea" was one of the first LPs he had owned in his bachelor days and was played over and over with friends about or when he was by himself and needed some company.

Erroll Garner's life story charmed Andy. Born a twin in June, 1923 he started playing the piano at age three. Early on he could hear something played and then

147

play it himself. An ear player he never learned to read music. He was performing by the time he was seven and by eleven was playing on the Allegheny riverboats. He was only five foot two inches tall and early on played sitting on a stack of telephone books. He died in January, 1977 at the age of fifty-three. He would often vocalized while he played as is heard on the Concert by the Sea album which was recorded live in a school assembly hall in Carmel-by-the-Sea, California. The master of ceremonies at the end of the concert calls him over asking, "Erroll. Erroll. Say a few words." He answers in a gravely voice, "It's worse than Louie Armstrong." One of his more famous quotes that Andy loved was whenever asked why he never learned to read music he answered with, "No one can hear you read."

It is Andy's thinking that this will be a fun project and he is eager to get underway. Garner had a marvelous African-American face accented with a rather large and broad nose, rounded checks, thin mustache and a great smile. Andy chose to do the bust with the smile, which ups the difficulty when working from photographs.

Turning on the stereo and putting on the headphones he started Concert and the first playing commenced. He had picked out three to memorize. *I'll Remember April, Teach Me Tonight, and Autumn Leaves* which are the first, second and fourth cuts on the CD.

He prepared the the armature and placed it on his sculpting stand. Forgetting to have turned on the clay heater and having to wait for the clay to soften he decided to finish cleaning up the piano bench. He had removed the leather cushion from the bench and after lining the studio's bath tub with plastic, carefully applied the paint remover to the wood surface with the bathroom vent running.

Unlike the piano, all the remaining lacquer and paint came off with one application and all that remained was some scrubbing and considerable sanding. Once that was done he patched the few scars and dents with a two part putty. He would sand them down later and mount the loose leg adding new bracing to all four. Andy was hoping he would be able to get a quality black finish with aerosol spray paint and lacquer. There was an upholstery shop a few blocks away on Fourth Street and he had already made arrangements with them to make the new leather seat cushion. In a week he would be playing his piano properly seated.

The clay had softened and he got the Garner CD playing from the start and it was coming in clear through the headphones. Andy was in a comfortable place and was again working fast. Listening to Garner brought some good memories of an earlier time when life seemed to have been much simpler.

He built up the head and the basic shape of Erroll was coming about. When the head shape was about right it was time for a break.

He walked up to 4th Street around the corner of Patterson's place. The window displays had sculptures of his and also a number by several of his family members. A mega site of bronze sculpture. Upstairs in his two buildings five more sculptors had their studios and there also was a private apartment. In the six block length of the street there were a dozen more studios and businesses that catered to the local sculptors. The bronze art business was, when taken as a whole, fast becoming the second largest business operation in Loveland, only exceeded by Hewlett Packard. It was a nice walk for a short break.

Returning to the studio it was back to work, listening to Erroll, and sculpting a likeness of him. Sometime around four Andy found himself in another strange moment as the music had stopped and he was just sitting on his stool looking at a rather large flat nose on a smiling face. "Not again. What's going on up there?" he asked himself tapping his his head with his knuckles. He remembered his short walk at mid-morning and getting started but from that time until just now, nothing. The progress on Erroll was such that it had been a very productive four or five hours but he couldn't remember any of it. He was hopeful the music had been memorized. He sensed it was but that would have to wait to be tested.

Andy closed up the studio bidding the boys good night and headed home. Something was going wrong with him which he thought he should tell someone about. Jan should know, of course, but not yet. He felt fine, his eye sight was great and he had good balance. He knew where he was, where he was going and how to get there. He went home.

CHAPTER 38

When Andy pulled into the driveway Jan's car was not there but that was not unexpected as her hours in real estate were never regular. He entered the town home by the front door, as it seemed to him a waste of electricity to open and close the garage door all the time, but his first move was into the garage. Uncovering the piano was his second. He sat in front of the Keyboard, lifted the Fallboard into it's place and then placed his hands on the Music Shelf.

The sensation is present and it comforts him knowing that another day has past and he still has this strange contact with this beautiful object. He thinks of Erroll Garner, places his hands over the keys and then hits those special chords that define Garner's first notes for *I'll Remember April.* He plays through it in style and with a smile of satisfaction continues through the first five cuts of the Concert By The Sea CD. It feels so good and so easy that he thinks only of the music.

Jan arrived home, and as she too has made the habit of entering through the front door, she walks up to it and enters the house. She can hear the Garner melody playing in the garage so she sets her briefcase and purse on the dryer and opens the door into the garage. Just as

151

she was about to call out a greeting to Andy she sees that it is him playing the piano. "Oh my God," is her first thought and she sits down on the door step. A feeling of fear comes over her. "He has learned to play that damn piano." She waits for him to finish in silence.

Andy is now really into the fact that not only has he memorized Garner during that period he can't remember, but he had just played the first five cuts. He starts over and plays them a second time. "This is really something. I will have to look in the mirror and make sure I am not Erroll Garner," he mutters aloud.

Jan couldn't restrain herself any longer and almost shouts out, "Andy, what are you doing? How are you doing that? How long have you being doing this?" She starts shaking and then the tears come. "What's going on, Andy? You have to tell me! Andy, you have to tell me!"

Andy jumped up when he hears Jan's first question and turns toward her. He stays some what bent over as he begins to come back to reality. Seeing Jan in such distress he knows it is time to tell her what is happening. Going over to her he reaches out for her hands and lifts her to her feet. "Let's go inside and have a long talk. It's time for me to tell you."

They sat close together on the couch. Andy puts his arm around her shoulders and gives her a gentle hug. "Jan, I have been listening to several different piano CDs trying to memorize every note played. The single notes, each note in the chords, how they are struck, the rhythm, tempo, whether dampened or not. Memorizing every bit of information I can." Jan acknowledged what he was saying by a weak nod and tries to get closer, but didn't speak.

Andy continued, "Right after Steve Pardee had the

piano tuned and adjusted, after Stefanie played that first night the piano was ready, I knew I must learn to play. I told you about this compulsion some time ago. Even before then I had secretively been playing the keys with the Action just on the bench. There was no sound of course, but I felt a confidence growing that I would be able to learn how to play. I knew I must learn. It was like a commandment. The first time I touched the keys I was able to play the first notes of *Rhapsody* without thinking about what I was doing. I couldn't believe it was possible, didn't think it was, and couldn't tell anyone what I was up to. "

Andy paused, but Jan didn't speak or even indicate she had heard what he was saying, so he continued, "What I did next was to press the keys individually over and over, firm, soft, hard, damped and not damped. I then tried to memorize some short combinations. The first was more of *Rhapsody in Blue*. I could do it so I then memorized *Clair de lune*. I can play it now. All of it. It was while I was memorizing *Clair de lune* that I sculpted the bust of Debussy." Again Jan was silent.

"I tried to tell you why this is possible before, you know that time in the wee hours of the morning after Stefanie played the piano the first time. You didn't believe me then."

"I don't believe it now. Tell me again. Make me understand. Make me believe it. Please." Jan asked but couldn't meet his gaze. She just stared down at her hands, clasped tightly in her lap.

"It started the first time I touched the piano. At the auction that Bill and I went to. I would never had made that bid if it hadn't happened then. Who knows what would have happened to the piano if I hadn't bought it but

I would never had called it out to the auctioneer if I hadn't sensed that feeling."

"I know," Jan almost pleaded. "I know there had to be a reason you would buy it, Andy, but was it really that. That's what I can't believe."

Andy would try again to explain. "That first time I touched it on the curve of the Case I felt the dust, grime, the wood and then it was almost like touching your arm." he said as he moved his free hand onto to her wrist with a light massage. "Just like that. Like the wood was warm and alive."

"I took my hand away and then placed it back onto the same spot and held it there." Andy squeezed her arm harder. "The auction noise went to quiet and the lights seemed dim. It scared me. I did it once more and the same thing happened. I was sure that the piano was sending me a message."

"That can't be, Andy."

"It was. No one else seems to feel it. I asked Bill to try, and also Jason. They couldn't feel it. It just comes up through my hands, then up my arms and into my chest. I can't describe it exactly but it is a good feeling, a feeling of confidence, of comfort."

"Are you sure? Absolutely sure this happens?"

"Yes, Jan. Every time I touch that piano." Andy then added. "When I am ready to play I just put my hands on the Music Shelf, get that sensation, and I can start playing knowing the piano will get me through the piece. It's magical."

They sat together without speaking for several minutes. Finally Jan asked. "Is that what happened to Stefanie when she played for us that night? Why she was crying and carrying on about love at first sight and loosing it?"

"Yes. For what ever reason the piano gave her permission to play at the highest level."

"Andy, that is crazy talk."

"Maybe so, but something happened there and everyone knew it."

Andy hugged Jan tighter and then she looked him in the eyes. "This is just something I will have live with for now. I still can't, won't, believe it can be true but I will live with it. Don't you leave me, Andy Miller. Don't you dare leave me."

Andy thought no one could believe a story like this but he did because it was happening to him. He understood what Jan was thinking. Anyone would think that. Only Stefanie would have even the remotest idea of what was going on and she didn't have a clue. He decided he had said enough for now and would keep his other problem to himself hoping it didn't become even worse.

CHAPTER 39

Jan's first words to Andy as they awakened the next morning were "I want to believe you." She rolled over to encircle him in a tight embrace. "I want to believe you. You can play that piano. There is no way you could do that unless something, or someone, was helping you. No someone could help that much so it must be the something else. I have to just accept the something else."

Jan jumped out of bed and promised breakfast in fifteen minutes. Andy felt a little better about the explanation he gave last night but he knew it wasn't rational. He would leave it be for a while as he wasn't sure what more he could say. At least he had been honest. The other problem would just have to wait. He had Erroll to take care of and Dave Brubeck was going to be next. Then Rachmaninoff, a real challenge, would follow.

He was eager to get the five finished as he wanted to start the plans to have a public concert and see if he could actual perform at that level under those conditions. Andy was sure it was the memorization that was causing him the problem of forgetting. It seemed effortless to do but thinking like an engineer he wondered if his memory bank was filling up. How much musical details can you memorize and retain? He was hoping he wouldn't find out.

In the studio Andy decided to use the speaker system to listen to Erroll and he would try to finish the bust by tomorrow. The sculpting seemed to be going slow but it was progressing. Doing the exposed teeth and the lips in a smile is hard to do but he had what he wanted in a couple of hours. It was on to do the the eyes and ears and by late afternoon he was satisfied with them. He was close to finishing so he closed up the studio and headed home feeling he had put in a good day.

Jan was there when he came in and gave him a kiss and a smile. They had a nice evening and took a short walk south on Taft Avenue. On the North West corner of Taft and eighth Street was Jane Goodwin's compound. She started out working for George Patterson, did a few sculptures of her own, developed a unique style and then hit the big time. Walking by one could often catch a glimpse of the activity inside and see a number of life size works in various stages of completion.

Jan turned to Andy. "Do you ever think of achieving that level in sculpture?"

"No!" \was Andy's quick response.

"Why not?"

"A number of things. It is a little late in life for me. I don't have that special thing that you need to develop a distinctive style. I am not a salesman. I like to work alone. Maybe not even the ambition."

"That quite a list, Mr. Miller," Jan responded in a good natured way. "But you are probably right. You need all those attributes to get there, don't you? Besides, we've had a pretty good life together so far. Might not work out if you were my boss."

157

"Sometimes you amaze me with your intuition."

They headed back up Taft holding hands, both somewhat lost in their own thoughts. Andy thinking about his next work with Dave Brubeck and Jan hoping this thing with the piano wouldn't end up badly.

Andy finished up Garner the next day. He thought Erroll looked pretty damn good. The look was just right. Despite what must have been a tough life his smile was genuine and conveyed a certain look of satisfaction. Andy thought he had done Erroll proud.

The piano bench was ready to spray paint. It was down to the parking lot with the bench, spray cans and a tarp. Andy had placed three inch screws into the bottom of the legs such that he would have them clear of the tarp. It was windless day and the lot was empty. Spreading the tarp he placed the bench upside down in the middle of it and proceeded to spray a series of thin coats of gloss black lacquer on the insides of the legs and the bench box. Carefully he righted the bench and sprayed all the exterior using the same technique. In thirty minutes the lacquer was dry to the touch, he carried the bench back up to the studio, then made a second trip for the tarp and paint cans. A fine sanding and second coat would be made, then sanding and coating with clear gloss lacquer would be repeated several times and then the bench would be ready for the new black leather cushion. Andy was sure this would work out as planned and was ready to return the dinning room chair to the dinning room.

It was early afternoon as Andy closed up his studio. It was so quiet downtown this day he thought he might have missed something important. He wasn't even sure what day it was. All he knew was that tomorrow would be the start of Dave Brubeck.

Andy moved Erroll over next Claude and George. "How about some company, you two?" Andy positioned them in an arc this time facing toward the studio's door. "Erroll, you are a handsome man." Andy thought he now had three new friends and soon there would be two more. He better make sure they get along together and also he better not be talking to them if anyone else is around.

A smile crossed Andy's face and he headed home.

CHAPTER 40

The next week was for Dave Brubeck. He was much more akin to Andy. Brubeck was born in December 1920, making him about fifteen years older than him, and was still living. His father was a cattle rancher and his mother a pianist who once wanted to play at the concert level but raising three boys had settled for teaching piano. Brubeck's two older brothers went into music while he was planning to go into the cattle business with his father. As fate sometimes dictates, all three boys ended successful in music but Dave's abilities to play and compose led him to be the more famous.

Brubeck's formal training was somewhat troubled by the fact that he couldn't sight read music. When that was discovered in college he was only allowed to continue as long as he promised not to ever teach music. He didn't have to as it turned out. In the service during World War II he was assigned to start and manage a band which occupied him through out the duration.

All this appealed to Andy's senses and adding to that he was a tall six footer, slender of build, and had a great smile. Andy held out the thought that maybe someday they might meet. He wasn't prepared to try for a meeting in regard to doing the sculpture and he would depend on the many photographs that were available. Also in doing a likeness of a person is fraught with legal issues if the sculptor makes any attempt to sell or use it for profit.

Andy picked the look from a photo of Brubeck at about 40 years of age with a big, open mouth smile, wearing large, dark rimmed glasses and a sport coat over a dress shirt sporting a very narrow tie. Cool was the pose. What the composer and player of *Take Five* would have looked like in 1960.

Anxious to get started Andy set up his sculpture stand, gathered the photos, and loaded his Time Out CD. With the headphones on, the Dave Brubeck Quartet in full swing, he was ready and the first handfuls of soft clay were being formed on the armature. Dave Brubeck was in the house.

The morning went by fast. Too fast in fact as late afternoon arrived and Andy's empty stomach final finally reached him with its message that food was required. He removed the headphones and looked carefully at his work. It was much further along than he had planned. The shape, the pose, and the detailing lines were in place. He picked up the largest copy of the photograph he had chosen and compared it to what he had done. It was spot on. Two days work in less than one day. He sat on his stool and stared at Dave. He looked over at Claude, George, and Erroll. They all looked back and Andy was sure he could see in their eyes interest in what he was doing.

At that moment he couldn't remember anything after the first handful of clay. Nothing. He sat motionless for another half hour then rose and slowly began closing up the studio. He had felt so alive and ready to start this piece. So ready for a day of Brubeck's cool jazz. "What is happening to me?" he said out loud. "Am I losing it?"

Jan was home when Andy got there. She gave him a smile and a questioning how's my best friend doing today look. "I had a good day. Brubeck is taking shape and I probably heard *Take Five* twenty times." was Andy's response to Jan's inquiry.

"Andy, you look tired. Sad. Is anything wrong?"

"I'm okay. Just a long day of concentration. I am going to see if the memorizing Brubeck is working. The CD is his quartet and there is a lot of dead time for the piano parts." And Andy was off into the garage.

"Dinner about six. One hour. Hear me, one hour." Jan thought she saw a nod but wasn't sure. She was starting to worry as Andy seemed to be drifting away. Nothing really apparent, just the feeling she had which was growing more worrisome. "Don't let this happen, don't let this happen," she whispered to herself.

Andy set up the piano and took his seat and positioned his hands on the Music Board. He let out a sigh as the sensation came on strong and his fingers hit the keys in the 5/4 time signature so familiar to Dave Brubeck's themes. *Take Five* came alive and then a unfamiliar bit of score occurred. Just as the first Paul Desmond's solo came Andy keeps the piano's dominate theme and adds some other notes and chords in the 5/4 time signature. They are common to *Take Five* but eliminates the constant piano background that accompanies the solo space. Shortly Andy does this again for both the bass and drum solos. It works seamlessly and keeps the mood through out.

Andy plays through *Take Five* a second time and it happens again. Jan had quietly entered the garage and took her seat on the doorstep. It was now onto *Blue Rondo A* La

Turk with its unusual different time signatures. 9/8 with odd groupings and sometime switching back to 4/4. Andy plays through it with covering the instrument solos in similar fashion as he did with *Take Five.*

Jan remained silent and was trying to understand what was different. The fact that Andy had covered for all the solo parts in this way wasn't even noticed by her as he played. When it dawned on her what had just happened her fear of what was going on with the piano grew and she felt helpless on what to do or say about it. She went back inside, quietly closing the door and putting his dinner on hold.

Art Myers

CHAPTER 41

Jan came back into the bedroom and gently shook Andy's shoulder. "It's nine Andy. I am going to the office and will be having lunch and playing bridge with my group. Should be home by four. Are you okay?"

"Yeah, I'm fine. Slept in I guess. I think I will take the day off," was Andy's groggy reply.

"I saw you ate the dinner I put out. What time did you come to bed?"

"About eleven-thirty. I did a lot of playing. I am comfortable with all the works I have memorized and actually added some parts in the Brubeck pieces. It surprised me that I could do that. As soon as I finish his sculpture I will start work on Sergei Rachmaninoff. When that's done I'm done."

This was news to Jan. "Done?"

"Well done as far as sculpting the busts and memorizing the music."

Jan sat down on the bed. "You better tell me what you mean by that!"

Andy was now wide a wake and knew it was the time to talk about the concert. This would either go over good with Jan or she would be one unhappy lady and it would probably ruin her day. It would not be a good day

164

to ruin, thought Andy.

"Okay, here's what I've been thinking. Once I am done and comfortable with my playing I would like to try it out in a public forum. If that is successful, we can decide how to proceed. Continuing on that route doesn't appeal to me so let's not worry about that option. Then the choice is keeping the piano, selling it, or sending it to a new home of our choice. If the concert doesn't work out we will have the same options. But I will be done with what I have been doing with the piano."

Jan looked at Andy and tried to decide what to say. The idea of a concert had never occurred to her but she was sure he had been thinking along those lines for some time. It was his mountain and he was climbing it because it was there.

"A concert? A real concert?" Jan asked trying to hide her surprise.

"Maybe at the Rialto Theater. Free. Our group could put the whole thing together. Maybe a hundred people would show up. It would give me the chance to see where I stood as a pianist. Just for my own ego, if you want. It is no crazier than the rest of this has been." The look on Jan's face told him what she was thinking at that moment. So he quickly added, "At least think about it. Okay?"

Jan got up and gave Andy the smile he needed. "You are crazy. But if that will end it I am all in. But please let it end," and she was out the door and Andy sat alone on the bed not sure this was working out exactly as he had planned.

After breakfasting and getting dressed Andy headed for the studio. He wanted to talk with Bill for a few minutes and he was going to call his two best galleries later as it had been months since his last contact.

Bill was there and Andy soon learned that he had been taking care of keeping the galleries up to date, taking the orders for the Bald Eagle sculpture and several of the smaller works. A true business manager. It turned out number eight and nine were in casting and six had been sold. Bill and Jan were taking care of the paper work and the money. And it also turned out Bill was now the hottest selling sculptor in both of Andy's galleries so he was happy.

Andy then went to his studio, said hello to the boys, picked up the now lacquered bench and headed to the upholstery shop. Some discussion on selection of seat foam, the choice of leather and setting the perfect height for Andy. The order was placed. One week from today.

Home by eleven Andy called his galleries and having good conversations with both meant he had covered the bases with time to spare. A quick lunch and it was into the garage.

The piano seemed to glisten in the muted light. The lid was up and it did not disappoint. He slid a hand along the rim as he walked around it. What a beautiful instrument. What a beautiful thing. It didn't matter if you played it or not. It was a work of art and the visual enjoyment should be enough. But it was meant to be played. Played with music to match it's beauty.

He sat down in front of the Keyboard and admired the keys. eighty-eight keys. What a nice number that was. He placed his hands on the Music Shelf and the sensation was there and he started to play. *Rhapsody, Clair de lune,* the three Garner works and Brubeck's two. Smooth as silk with no effort. They just flowed off his fingertips. What a feeling it gave him.

After two hours and about three complete playing of what he knew how to play he stopped. Andy just stared ahead and savored what he had just done. It felt so good he couldn't, and wouldn't, ever try to explain it to anyone. This could all end right now and he would have no regrets no matter which way fate would take it. In that moment he was happy beyond words.

CHAPTER 42

The preceding few weeks had been tough on Andy but he felt the end of this adventure was in sight. His confidence was growing that he could play his piano at a high enough level to perform in public. He had no problem accepting the fact that he could only do this on his piano and that once he did a concert his options for the future would narrow. Doing a tour was not going to happen. The needed self promotion and travel required was not in his DNA. He was at peace with this thinking and was also formulating solution that might just work.

It had taken Andy three days to finish the Brubeck sculpture. He had made two mistakes. The first was deciding that since his playing of his choices of Brubeck's work were so good he would finish the sculpture without the music in his ears. The second was his choice of the pose. He worked slowly this time and by the end of the day had it pretty much roughed in as he had planned but it didn't look right. The big open mouth smile was the problem. It didn't look cool as in the photograph he was using. In fact it looked goofy. It had been a long day. He was tired and disappointed with what he had done and decided to wait until tomorrow before trying to figure out what to do about it. This time he could remember every minute of the day's effort which he now wished he could forget.

On the second morning he asked Bill to take a look at Dave. "It doesn't work Andy. That big smile just does not work," was Bill's immediate and correct reaction.

"I know, I know," Andy said acknowledging the obvious. Making small corrections is generally not a difficult task but this was major as changing the mouth meant all the other facial features would have to be adjusted. Even worse was that Andy had done the teeth and lips really good which was not an easy task and he didn't want to waste that effort.

Andy then did things right. He turned on the stereo and Time Out was in full swing. He took one of his thin bladed knives and removed Brubeck's lower jaw. Adjusting it such that his smile was about half as open as before made an immediate improvement. A little more tweaking and Andy was back on the right track. The rest of the day flew by. He was happy with what he had done. It was still a big open mouth smile but this time it looked right and projected a happy and very cool Dave Brubeck.

He finished all the detailing the following day and by early afternoon Dave was ready to join the group. Andy then took the rest of the day off and did absolutely nothing.

"It is Sergei Rachmaninoff's turn," was Andy's thought as he entered his studio the next morning. But first he had a small project to take care of. He had a set of nesting pedestals that he displayed his sculptures on at art shows and he brought over five of them from the garage. He placed the bust's of Gershwin, Debussy, Garner, and the just finished Brubeck on four of the pedestals in an attractive arrangement, including the fifth pedestal for the soon to be sculptured Rachmaninoff bust. After some additional adjustments Andy thought the group made an impressive display. It gave him the sense of having company.

He had his clay heater running and set up his sculpture stand and an armature. The Rachmaninoff No. 2 CD was in the player and he pushed the repeat play button and seated himself on the wheeled stool.

But first he reviewed what he had read about Sergei. He had lead some kind of life. He was born in Russia in March of 1873 into a musical family. A family of aristocracy and substantial means thanks to his mother's dowry of five estates when she married his father. Unfortunately it was reduced, due his father's financial incompetence, gambling, and other passions, to just one by the time he had reached the age of ten.

His piano and music lessons, organized by his mother, began when he was four. The family had moved to the last remaining estate in Saint Petersburg and with his ability to memorize, and his musical talent, lead him to the Conservatory there where his formal teaching occurred. Some of his father's traits seemed have reached his son and later he was forced by them to transfer to the Moscow Conservatory. In any case he was taught and mingled with many of the greats of the time. By fifteen he was on the upward path of education and was composing and performing at the highest level.

He received his diploma from the Moscow Conservatory in the spring of 1892 and, in modern terms, could turn professional. He composed his Piano Concerto No. 2 in the first few years of 1900 and he was the soloist for it in a performance of the finished work in a competition in Paris in 1907. The award was presented to him as was a considerable payment. This brought him out of a ten year period of self doubt and depression. The activity that followed this success rivals that of any musician both in compositions and performances. The Russian Revolution of 1917 made part of his life Dr. Zhivago like at home and, other than that he was in constant movement and creativity, he knew it was time to leave Russia. Arriving in New York in 1918 he became a virtual business unto himself with composing, performing, conducting and guiding others. He died in March of 1943, in Beverley Hills, California, at seventy years of age. But what a seventy years it had been.

It was beyond Andy's comprehension that one man could have lived such a life. Just reading about it tired him out. It was now time for him to expend a little effort of his own. He plugged in the headphones and grabbed the first handful of clay.

Listening to *Piano Concerto No. 2* with orchestration it was hard for Andy to hear some of the piano parts clearly. The pauses in playing were defined but when as accompaniment it got a little muddled. At almost forty minutes there were several minutes that he couldn't quite catch everything. He decided to use the piano solo recording even though he liked the orchestra version a little better. Each playing brought what he needed to do come more into focus.

Andy worked on through the day and as with the other sculptures he was making much faster progress than he was used to accomplishing. The music was becoming more and more familiar. There were already a number of parts that he felt he had memorized. Again, like it had happened with Brubeck, he suddenly felt that he should stop for the day. He set down the tool he was using and looked about his studio and realized it was getting dark outside. The CD player automatically started to replay *No. 2* and he went back into a trance as he concentrated on it.

At the same time Jan had called Bill. When he answered she spoke quickly.

"Bill this is Jan. Andy hasn't come home yet and I am a little worried. He's always back by now and if he had something going on he would of called me. Could you check on him for me?"

"Sure will. I'm home but it will take just a minute. I'll call you right back."

Bill was at Andy's studio in a couple of minutes and Andy was in the exact position he was the last time he had dropped in on him. This time the player was on and again when Bill called out his name there was no response. Bill walked over and put his hand on Andy's shoulder, "Andy, it's Bill. You okay buddy?"

Andy slowly turned to face him and Bill could see his eyes start to focus and show recognition. "Hey buddy, you better lighten up on this working. Jan called and is worried about you. So am I."

"Ah. . . Ah. . . I'm ok. Just a little tired and I have really been concentrating on the music. This is a tough one."

Bill was worried but wanting the best for Andy said. "You best close up shop and get home to your mate. She's pretty worried about you not being home yet."

Andy smiled at that and asked Bill to call her and tell her he would be home in a few minutes. Thanking Bill he quickly shut the studio and the two of them went down the stairs to the street together.

CHAPTER 43

Andy climbed into his van and headed home driving his usual route. When he was about half way there an emotion of sadness overwhelmed him. Not since his father's funeral had he had this kind of feeling. He pulled over to the curb and started to sob. "What the hell is wrong with you? This is an adventure of a life time. It's going great. Jan, Bill, your new group of friends. Your piano." Andy couldn't shake the feeling of desperation. "Why? . . Why? Is it the music? Is it Rachmaninoff? Maybe you're just worn out trying to do something you know you shouldn't be able to do and afraid it will be suddenly taken away from you. Just like what happened to Stefanie."

That last thought seemed to calm him a bit and in a few more minutes the sadness began to slowly fade away. He tells himself, "Get over this before you let Jan see you." He needs her now, more than ever, but he can't let her in on this last bit. He is so close to finishing what he wants to accomplish with the piano. When it is done, or more likely over, he will have no regrets and will get back to a normal life. "I can do this. I know I can do it," and he pulls out into the street and continues the trip home.

Jan is waiting for him and she gives him a close

look and ask, "Andy are you okay? Is everything alright?"

"Yes to both." Andy's smile is a little weak but his voice is steady and he reaches out for a comforting embrace. Jan still has doubts but thinks it is best to let that pass, at least for now.

"I was a little worried so I called Bill. Hope you don't mind. You have spoiled me by always letting me know about any change in your schedule so when you didn't show up I was afraid something had happened to you."

"Not a problem. It was good to see Bill. He caught me with the headphones on and listening to Rachmaninoff. I just lost track of time."

Jan gave Andy a smile and said "Dinner is ready."

After dinner they wasted some time watching television and then headed for bed around ten, which was a little late by their current habit. As was the norm Jan was asleep in minutes but Andy, as tired as he had been in weeks, was wide awake. He laid there thinking of his day. It had started as planned and with a good deal of optimism. From that point on he could not remember a thing until Bill tapped him on the shoulder. Then there was that episode on the drive home. It was going to be hard to fall asleep and he was right. About one-thirty it came.

Jan was up first, but they had breakfast together and both left the house about nine. Andy was in the studio fifteen minutes later and made a careful inspection. Sergei was waiting and was looking pretty good for a guy with no nose or ears and just a couple of marble shape clay eyes. No hair didn't help his appearance either. Andy told him, "You will be much happier by days end, my man."

Andy had hundreds of photos to choose from. Many were from live shots but most were studio ones. The man never smiled. The studio photos had been carefully posed. Added to the references were photos of a number of paintings, a couple of record jacket covers, one showing off his large hands with fingers spread, and even photos of a couple of sculptures. Almost all showed the exact same features, the only real difference was his age. Andy choose one at the time he was around fifty as his primary reference.

He put on the CD but not the headphones. He knew he would probably work at a slower pace but he wanted to test how this would affect the memory problem. He spent a full day and by its end he had the bust almost complete. The hair was yet to be sculpted and the fine detailing remained including defining the coat and tie. Otherwise Andy was pleased with what he had done.

He walked up Fourth Street to the upholstery shop to see how they were doing with the bench and found it was done. They were so proud of their work they had a mini unveiling for him, pulling a dark red piece of yardage off it with a flourish. Sitting in the middle of their workroom it seemed to cast off an aurora of elegance. Andy stepped over to it, sat down with a proper posture and his smile told the owners they had succeeded. It was so comfortable that his smile was a combination of being totally pleased with its look and its feel. He moved about a bit and the firmness was just right to allow for that movement. It was perfect.

Andy carried it back down 4th Street to his studio high up on his shoulder and got the many admiring looks he anticipated. After closing up the studio and returning home he placed the bench in the middle of the living room. He was going to wait until tomorrow, after Sergei had taken his place with his new friends, to put it in front of the piano and test it for its fit and himself for Rachmaninoff. It had been a good day and Andy felt much better than he had the day before.

Andrew's Piano

CHAPTER 44

As the afternoon shadows appeared outside the studio windows Andy was doing the finishing touches on Sergei. His hair was shown cut short in the photo he was using and he had a distinctive hair line. Andy was very satisfied in his treatment of the hair adding only a few minor texture lines. He had the nose, ears and eyes right and the lips were correct but there was no humor in the man. A little more work on the corners of the mouth got just what he was looking for, a hint of amusement. That minor change made the difference. It made the eyes look better without needing any adjustments.

Andy spent the next half hour circling Sergei carefully examining everything he had done. "Okay Sergei, I am done with you and it is time to take your place with your new friends. You be nice, you hear. Remember, Debussy died the same year you came to America and even if he was French you should be able to get along. Gershwin was just getting started when you passed away and I suppose you wouldn't have ever heard of Brubeck or Garner. Just let the music be your bond."

When Andy had placed Sergei on his pedestal he made a few adjustments to the display and then stood back for a long appraisal. "They look good, really good together," was his thought.

He closed up the studio and headed home. After a short detour to pick up the bench it was straight into the garage. When Jan had come home from work yesterday and saw the refurbished bench she said to Andy "Look what you have done with that dumpster dive find. It's beautiful."

"Sit on it. Feel the leather."

She did and let out a very sexy sigh and stroked the leather. "Oh my, I better not sit here much longer."

"Maybe you should," was Andy's suggestion.

But it was now time to find out how the big test with Rachmaninoff would turn out. The sculpture was a success, the new bench was in place, and Andy placed his hands on the Music Shelf. It was there. As powerful as he had ever felt the sensations. He then positioned his hands and started Piano *Concerto No.2 - Solo Piano*, the First Movement. The single notes and chords came out perfect building up to the more expressive parts. It was thrilling to Andy that he could do this. Jason had said, "You can't do that!" but he was. Not only he was, but it was so good he could feel goose bumps on his arms.

Right through to the final chords, only a moment was allowed to adjust to the start of the Second Movement, and then through it and into the Third. It was magic. Just over thirty-five minutes of the best Andy had ever played. He needed to rest now and if he could do it again it would be time to plan a concert to bring this marvelous adventure to some kind of conclusion.

His rest break lasted only fifteen minutes and he had to try it again. The result was the same, maybe even better. When he finished he felt exhausted but the excitement was so high he was just about to play through it one more time when he heard Jan's voice from behind him. She was sitting on the step. "Andy, my God Andy, that was great. How can you possible play like that?"

"Did you hear it from the start?"

"Yes, Andy . . .Ah . . ." she couldn't think of what to say.

"Rachmaninoff is something else, isn't he? This piece is so good. I am not ready to lose this yet. The piano has got to let me finish this thing off. I want to have the concert, and the sooner the better."

Jan stood up and on shaky legs walk over to Andy and put her arms around him, holding his back to her.

"Andy, I will do whatever you want on this. Call it whatever you want. Even if I don't believe this can be happening lets get it done. What ever you want. What ever you want."

"Lets get the team together and make the plans for the concert. Let's do it here, around the piano."

Jan was true to her word and the get together was set for the night after next, six o'clock sharp, around the piano, pot luck. Everyone was excited and couldn't wait to be part of it and make it happen.

When the eight good friends were gathered in the garage, surrounding the piano, Andy gave a short speech. "Most of you know something is going on here that shouldn't be. Namely, I shouldn't be able to play this piano, any piano, like I can right now. Also the reason I am able to is not rational. I know that and I want it to be clear to each of you. What has happened is best described as magical, super natural, or mystical and like those things can disappear at any second. That's the risk we take in planning a concert. So it should be free and presented as a maybe performance."

"What are you talking about?" Bill asked, with Julia, Ron and Roberta nodding their heads in agreement.

Andy continued, almost like he hadn't finished his former point. "This piano has some kind of magic that allows me to play like I knew what I was doing. I have memorized all the music I intend to play at the concert. I can play it all, but I really don't know what I am doing. It just happens! And that magic could just disappear at any time. It has been with me since I first touched the piano at the auction and I am hoping it will let me perform at the concert. That is the risk."

There were some questioning looks going about and then Stefanie came to the rescue. "I know what Andy is talking about. That night I played the piano, right here in the garage for you. The first playing. It happened to me. It was magic. I can't explain it any other way. Magic. And then it was gone. It was terrible to lose that feeling. The feeling that you cannot make a mistake. Just play the music. Then to have it gone"

Jason looked around and said "Let's plan the concert just like Andy wants. Free and no guarantee."

CHAPTER 45

The team filed back into the house and the plates were loaded. Lots of talk on several subjects but mostly on ideas on how to do the concert. After desert, which Jan had made and most had seconds of, the real work began. It started so easily that it was a foregone conclusion that this could be done and done the right way.

Stefanie offered that she had organized several of the High School music events at the Rialto Theater. The rent was reasonable, the staff helpful, and the Theater had everything that was needed technically to put on a performance. She knew all the people involved and would do the co-ordination to rent the venue. Where to have it was decided.

Ron put forth the idea of recording the concert and that he had all the equipment needed and would be happy to set everything up. Stefanie offered more help in that she had worked with the staff on both sound and lighting and was sure they would set up the theater's system and would not only let Ron set up his but would even assist him.

Andy ventured that he wanted to position the piano the day of the concert and bring it back the next day. As few people as possible touching it before the concert was best and he would be supervising that part. He was worried about the magic if that made any sense. But that was it. Why he didn't want unfamiliar hands touching his piano. Bill let out a little knowing chuckle and received a sharp elbow in the ribs from Julia.

Jason and Roberta offered any help they could. Roberta would look into legal problems that might come up though she didn't think there should be any.

There was a lot of discussion as to the date, time, how many to expect, whether to have tickets or not. All were excited and thrilled with the idea of the event. Andy felt a slight unease as he was losing control of events but understood that the time had come and if he was to pull this off he had to let go. He felt good that everyone here wanted him to succeed.

Julia then commented on the sculptures Andy had done and why not arrange them on the stage. Half the people that would come to this would know sculpture and if placed and lit correctly it would be worth their while to come just to see the them. She was given the best suggestion of the evening award.

The planning carried on for a while longer and it was decided that a week night would probably work out best because the Theater had a fairly busy Friday, Saturday and Sunday programs. It was decided to try for a Wednesday or Thursday, Thursday preferred. The time should be 8:00 PM. Andy indicated the playing time would be about one hour. Julia remarked you better be ready with an encore.

It would be free. Word of mouth and maybe one article in the Reporter Herald the week before. Roberta would take care of that. She knew several of the staff at the paper.

Andrew's Piano

Andy volunteered as the evening was getting late that he would try to play his latest for them. That he was still tweaking it a bit but it was ready to go. All were ready for this and immediately crowded into the garage. Those who just had the magic explained were all eyes and ears. Those who knew what coming were relaxed and ready.

Andy took his seat, smiled at his friends and placed his hands on the Music Shelf. It was there and was strong. He positioned his hands and then gave them Rachmaninoff's *Piano Concerto No. 2*, all three movements, in about as good as it could be played. They were stunned. Only Jan had heard him play it before, and even she was without words when he finished.

Finally Julia spoke. "That is true magic. I think that is the best thing I have ever heard. Ever"

That was enough said and the team said their good nights. Each knew as they left the garage that their lives, in one way or another, had been changed that night.

CHAPTER 46

The planning for the concert had come to be and all was in place. The second Thursday after the team had met was reserved at the Rialto Theater. Gus, no other name, was signed up for sound and lighting and all else needed. The piano was brought over by Andy, Bill and Ron in a cube van with an hydraulic lift and with some engineering was now sitting stage center on a fine twelve by sixteen foot dark red carpet, slightly angled with the keyboard stage left. The bench was in place. The five sculptures were on Andy's pedestal which were draped with black and arrange in a semi-circle arc stage right.

Gus took care of the lighting with a flood over the piano which would cast a soft, almost gold, light in a circle on and around it. An interior light was placed in the Case. He then set a flood over the sculptures which would provide just enough soft white light to make them ghost like during the performance. When each each work was played a spot would highlight the related individual sculpture. The theater had been darkened and the lighting tested. It was much better than good.

Gus then set up the sound system. Two microphones strategical placed on stands at either end of the piano's Case. He let Ron place his two mikes adjacent to the theater's. The cables ran under the carpet to a port in the floor and then under the stage to the control booth and out to the first row of seating for Ron's tape recorder. All was tested. The theater volume was set for hearing piano music. Ron thoroughly tested his equipment and his was also ready.

Gus would be in the theater until the last person had left tonight. Some people are indispensable. Stefanie told the team he would be and that he knew what he was doing. All the team agreed on that assessment.

At seven-thirty the time had come and the Rialto Theater doors were opened. It was just over a year since since Andy had placed his hand on that dust covered piano body at the IRS auction. His and Jan's marriage was still intact, his friendship with Bill still sound and both of them were with him seated on the stage left in the wings. In the front row were Julia, Ron, Stefanie, Jason and Roberta. All new and best friends to Andy and Jan and all involved in the best of ways in their lives. Two others joined the group and they were Steve and Sandra Pardee who didn't want to miss this event and had flown in from Indiana that afternoon.

Jan was close to having an emotional breakdown and Bill was almost as nervous with hands shaking and perspiration forming on his forehead. Andy, however, for the first time in months felt calm. At peace with himself and actually was looking forward to what was about to happen. It had surprised him that he felt this way but was grateful he did. He had just placed his hand on the Music Shelf and the sensation was there and immediate. That was the sign he needed. He was sure he could do his part.

As the first patrons took their seats, Gus started

dimming the house lights and the piano at stage center then became the impressive focus. The sculptures were sufficiently lit to balance the view but didn't detract from sight of the beautiful Steinway Grand Piano. This was a free concert with no program or handout. It had been word of mouth with but one small article, written by Roberta, in the week-end Reporter Herald. Those that knew Andy had come early and soon filled the first few rows of the 450 seat theater. Most of the town's sculptors, a large number of the foundry hands and artisans, a number of the local painters, and many of the supporting business members were present. Other social friends, acquaintances and most of Jan's real estate partners and contacts had also shown up. Surprisingly the hall filled quickly and the front doors had to be closed a few minutes before the scheduled start.

Onstage were just the threesome. Jan and Bill seated next to each other out of sight and Andy standing nearby. At eight o'clock sharp Gus blinked the house lights three times then slowly dimmed them to semi-darkness. Andrew's piano literally glowed under the flood light with it's glossy black lacquer finish and the soft golden reflection from inside the Case reflecting off the underside of the open Lid. The anticipation in the theater was suddenly almost a physical presence. Something was happening at this moment that was very new for all that were present.

Andy had been standing backstage next to Jan and had been observing the arrivals and seemed to be in a special place. He was dressed in dark slacks, a white dress shirt and wore polished black loafers. Jan had put out his clothes but was still surprised that he had dressed and groomed so carefully. He seemed so confident and not even anxious. Professional was what came to her mind and that was not what she had expected. The opposite of that was what she had been fearing. But as if cued by a manager Andy strode out onto the stage to light applause, smiling at the house, then slowly circled the piano letting his hand slide along the smooth surface of the rim. As he reached the far end of the piano he turned toward the sculptures and nodded to them. He then completed the circle, assumed his position in front of the Keyboard, and sat down on the bench as the most gifted of pianist would have done. He adjusted the bench slightly and placed his hands on the Music Shelf.

CHAPTER 47

Andy knew at that moment all would go well. Confidence filled him as it never had before. He brought his arms down, positioned his hands and fingers, and then struck the first notes and chords of the familiar beginning of Gershwin's *Rhapsody in Blue*. The clear sound and perfect tone, along with the atmosphere, was such that an audible gasp came from the audience, as if all in the hall took in a breath at the same time. Jan started to quietly sob and tears were cascading down her cheeks. Bill, noticing, moved quickly to put his arm around her shoulders and held her tight. A year of extreme stress and doubt were suddenly coming undone for her. All at once the hours and hours of Andy's time and the seemingly constant time he spent in the garage was coming out as he performed a polished and beautiful rendition of this most well known and popular piece.

The soft spotlight was on Andy's sculpture of George Gershwin and if one had looked very closely you might have detected a slight smile. At least one could wish for that.

In the second row center sat Charles Perkins, a professor of music at the University of Colorado, who hadn't wanted to attend but had been forced to by his girl friend, an old friend of Jan and Andy, Joan Wilson. His first thought was, "Oh My God, not Rhapsody," but then he almost immediately sensed something else and started to listen carefully. Something was different, but he could not place what is was.

The audience had gone completely silent. Each note seemed almost perfect, the rhythm, chords, changes in tempo, the melodies and themes familiar to many came over just as they should and for those few unfamiliar were offered a new experience they would treasure.

Just as the final notes of *Rhapsody* were starting to fade away Andy leaned forward and said, just loud enough to be heard, "Dave. Dave Brubeck. Do you have some time?" and it was into the immediately recognizable *Take Five* with Brubeck's time signature 5/4 cadence. Andy filled in all the solo parts of the Quartet's composition with takes from other riffs or just skipped over them. It was a delightful rendering after the big music of *Rhapsody*. He followed up with *Blue Rondo A La Turk* with all it's idiosyncrasy. It was cool jazz as it was meant to be played. Brubeck in clay was spot lighted and his characteristic big smile looked bigger than ever.

Again Andy allowed no time for applause as he asked, "Erroll. Erroll are you there?" and he was into the playing the odd set of chords that introduces *I'll Remember April*. He played as Erroll Garner played, big rolling chords carrying the melodies and with quick fingering notes for accents. Andy was playing as Garner played in his Concert By The Sea recording and added *Teach Me Tonight* and *Autumn Leaves* in quick succession. Before the last of the Garner chords died, and while the Garner sculpture was still lit showing one great guy's great smile,

189

Andy announced, "It's time for Debussy," and the first notes of the classical and softer *Clair de lune* filled the theater. The audience went totally silent as every note demanded their attention. *Clair de lune, Moonlight* if you will, is one piece that can make you fall in love with a piano and a number in the hall did just that. That Debussy, that rascal, knew how to use music and he was a master. The sculpture of Debussy showed little interest in what Andy was playing but surely had to approve of how it was played.

One more time as Andy finished *Clair de lune*, hesitating for just a moment, he whispered the name "Sergei Rachmaninoff," followed by, "It's your turn." For the next thirty-four minutes he played the three movements of Rachmaninoff's *Concerto No. 2 - Solo Piano*. There were no breaks between the movements as he used a few chords and fingering to make the links. It was the best of his performance and he knew he had performed it right. He put his hands down, bowed his head slightly, and looked over at Sergei who remained in the spotlight. Andy was sure he saw the edges of his mouth twitch such that it could have been a start of a smile. That was all Andy needed to see.

This time Charles Perkins's, "Oh My God!" was heard by many.

The applause started and grew louder and louder. Andy slowly walked over to Jan who was now standing, along with Bill, adding their applause to the rest. He suddenly felt tired and a feeling of depression was welling up in his mind. He looked into Jan's eyes and told her, "I need to go home." He paused and then told her, "I think I am done."

Andrew's Piano

"Andy you were great! Great! Listen to that applause. They want more, Andy." She was so full of pride she missed the look in his eyes and continued, "Andy they want more. Listen to the applause. You have to at least take a bow and thank them. You have to!"

Andy looked back over his shoulder, saw the house standing and then began hearing for the first time the applause. He looked at Jan for a moment, then turned and slowly walked back on stage. As he neared the piano and came back into the flood lit space the applause increased and the call for more took over.

CHAPTER 48

Andy sat down on the bench and spread out his hands on the Music Shelf. He could feel the familiar sensations, they were again strong, and at this moment he really needed them. The applause had abated, the call for more ceased, and the house waited. He smiled, then leaned forward and spoke in a soft yet clear voice.

"I have to confess to you that I have played for you every piece I know. I don't know how to read music. I have never played any instrument before. As some of you are aware I bought this piano at an auction a year ago and spent a lot of time on it's restoration. All the while it has had some kind of hold on me. And it still does. Once it was playable I seemed to be able to press the right key for whatever sound I wanted. Even the multiple keys for the chords, know how to place my hands and fingers and what pressures to apply. Even the use of the pedals was intuitive. What I have played tonight were the works I have memorized from recordings. I thank you for liking what I have had to offer."

The quiet extended as the audience tried to interpret what Andy had just said. It didn't make sense to most and there was some murmuring but it was then quickly followed by more applause and a modest chant of "play it again" commenced. Andy positioned his hands and picking parts from his earlier offerings entertained them for another half hour.

He then stood up, turned to face the audience, smiled and gave a wave. He headed back to Jan and Bill. This time Jan led Andy off the stage and out the back exit to their car. On the short drive to the town home she kept asking, "What's happening?"

Andy responded "I can't tell you right now. I am not sure I know. I've tried to explain it to you a number of times but the words don't seem to help you understand what happens when I touch the piano. But it is over. I am now done."

Jan glanced at him, his face lit by the street lamps, and for the first time since the piano had entered their lives she felt a closeness to Andy that had seemed to have been lost. She could wait until he tried to explain it to her again, what was going on. It had been some kind of evening and she now felt that maybe she had been wrong. Wrong about a lot of things. She had no idea of the force the piano had over him as it made no sense to her. She still had many questions, but they could wait.

Joan Wilson had punched Charles as he was again standing but not applauding and had the same totally lost expression on his face. She gave him a second look and he said "Let's get going and I will try to explain what I think just happened. Actually I don't really think I know but something is not right. What Andy explained seems like science fiction. I just don't know what to think at the moment."

Joan had seen Jan and Andy's departure and Charles's comment made her wince as looking around all the others in the hall seemed to have smiles on their faces and were again wildly applauding. She sensed something had happened that she didn't understand and Andy's short explanation seemed unbelievable. She had enough piano training over the years and with the last few years with Charles had attended many very high quality performances. She knew the effort and talent that was required to perform at this level. There was this feeling, however, as Charles spoke that there was something just a bit different in Andy's playing but it had seemed to her to have been excellent and the selection was just right for the audience. She thought really quite remarkable.

As they left the theater Charles told Joan, "You drive. I need to think." Which was somewhat redundant since it was her car and she had driven up from Boulder. As they turned South and left most of Loveland behind, Charles still hadn't spoken a word.

"Well?"

Charles grunted and said "I don't know. It's something."

"That's not a very good answer, Charles."

A few more minutes passed then Charles started, very carefully choosing his words. "His selection and order of play was excellent. His skill in playing was way better than average, in fact excellent, and he made no mistakes as far as I could tell. Everything was memorized, as he said, which is amazing when you think about how difficult that is to do. It was the sound of that piano that was different. The tone. Fantastic. I can't remember ever hearing anything like it. Also, each piece he played was as if it was played by the player he cited and those he didn't cite, each was just a bit different in style. That could have been

Garner or Brubeck at the keyboard but it wasn't canned. It was Andy playing. There was no way it could have been other than him. He even admitted how he memorized by playing recordings over and over. But it was the sound and tone more than the style that has me baffled."

Charles closed his eyes wanting desperately to hear each and every note again. That was it. It was the piano. It had to be the piano.

He asked Joan, "Could arrange something with Jan and Andy so I could take a close look at the piano and maybe even play it. I would like to know more about what I just witnessed. That was extraordinary. Unbelievable."

Charles was right in his thinking but wrong in his hope of finding out. He would get to examine and play the piano, that would happen later on, but he would never experience it's magic.

CHAPTER 49

Andy and Jan were home in a few minutes and entered their quiet space that seemed to be missing the warmth it should have. Andy was emotionally drained and the feeling of depression was descending on him in full force. Jan was on a high of pride and relief that he had performed beyond her wildest dreams.

They looked at each other while standing in the middle of the small living space. Andy was the first to speak. "Jan, I am done. It's over."

"What are you talking about. Andy that was a great performance. More than great. How can it be over? This should be the beginning, not the end."

Andy moved Jan to the couch and pulled up a chair to sit directly in front of her. "Jan, I want you to listen carefully to me. This is going to be hard to explain. I think I have got this right. Please, just listen."

He took her hands in his, looking directly into her eyes, told her what had happened and why. Before he started he prefaced it by telling her he knew she would think he was crazy but this was his conclusion and the only one he could come up with that made any sense.

"I have already told you about first touching the piano at the auction. If I hadn't experienced that sensation the piano would never had entered our lives and it could have been carelessly tossed out as junk, or maybe someone might have salvaged the parts and sold them off. It could even have been that another might have recognized the value and restored it. We will never know but what we do know was that I felt that contact and did what I did."

Andy paused and could tell Jan was still with him so he continued. "You have been a party to everything that followed. Not willingly at first, but a party to it. Our new friends, the team that formed, were the result of that piano. Julia we would have met through Bill and it may have turned out the Stevens would be part of our lives because of your finding the house for them, but I doubt they, or Julia, would have become such close friends. We would never have met the Roberts. The piano was the magnet." Again Andy paused to let this be part of what he was now getting ready to try to explain. Jan only nodded but Andy could see in her eyes that she was focusing on what he was saying.

"I think, even though I don't believe in fate, that what has happened had to be for some purpose. It wasn't because I was a musician, or loved music, or even that I did have the skills that could restore the piano. I think it was the piano's last chance to survive." The startled look in Jan's eyes told Andy what he was expecting. "Jan, that is crazy talk. I know that for sure but bear with me here. I need you to understand this next part and it may be even harder to accept."

Andy shifted his position a bit, leaned in closer to Jan and finished his thoughts. "I think that the ability to memorize the music must be in a part of my brain that has never been used. It was just there. That is not what is important. What I believe, at least now, is that the piano allowed me, gave me an undeserved ability, to be able to play that music. I have the eye hand coordination to do it, I have always had it, but never related to a musical instrument. To actually play, and confidently play, that music came from somewhere else. It had to be from the piano. It has to be something like that."

Andy again shifted position and squeezed Jan's hands even tighter. "I think that the permission, or gift, to play is now over."

Jan was speechless. She sat without moving, hardly breathing. Finally she stuttered out, "How do you know that? How do you know it is over?"

"I will know for sure tomorrow when I touch the piano. It won't be there. I am sure of it. Just as I was finishing the concert I could feel it slipping away. When the encore was to start it was granted me one more time but as it ended so did it. It was like turning a light off. Immediate."

"Oh Andy, that can't be true. You were so good, spectacular, that can't be the end. Not now. Not this way."

They sat in silence. Lost in what this could mean and what was to happen next. Andy then surprised Jan by asking if she had Ron's telephone number. She handed him the cell phone and said to punch six. On the fourth ring Ron answered.

"Hi Andy, you doing okay?"

"I'm fine. I have a question for you."

"And I have the answer. Great, absolutely great. Perfect in fact." Ron was almost giddy.

Andy wasn't surprised at this and told Ron he would see him tomorrow at the theater.

Jan was puzzled. "What kind of conversation was that?"

"Do you remember the night we had at the Stevens when they had the party to show off their addition to the house?"

"Of course."

"Do you remember on the way home you asked me what that room needed?"

"Yes!" was Jan's quick reply and her eyes brightened up.

"Do you remember my answer?"

"Andy is that what you are thinking?"

"Yes, again."

Art Myers

CHAPTER 50

The next morning Andy was at the Rialto at nine and found the back door near the loading dock unlocked. Entering, he went to the stage and Gus was seated on the piano bench with his back to the piano. "Hi Andy. I figured you would be first here. That's some piano you got."

"It sure is," Andy answered.

"Yes sir. I have heard a lot of piano playing in my time but that was something special last night. You had the audience. Had them completely. That doesn't happen to often. Seen it once a long time ago with one of your boys over there." Nodding in the direction of the sculptures. "Yeah, Dave Brubeck came to San Diego one night when one of his brothers, can't remember which one, was directing the San Diego Symphony at the outdoor amphitheater in Balboa Park. Starlight Bowl I think it was called. After the regular performance was done, Brubeck and his quartet was introduced and they started to play, probably *Take Five* just like you did last night. This maybe was 1953, 54 and the Starlight crowd was as square as could be. Like my Mom and Dad, who took me there. I was in high school but didn't know nothing about music. Well Brubeck got that crowd. They wouldn't let him go. More, we want more. He kept saying we got a plane to catch for

Andrew's Piano

San Francisco, but that bunch wanted more. He had them just like you had that bunch last night. That doesn't happen often. Andy, I am glad I was here."

"Thanks Gus. Stefanie said you were special and she was right on."

Gus looked around, then motioned Andy closer. "That Stefanie is something special. You mark my words."

Andy smiled at that and just then Ron and Bill came in from the back door. Greetings were exchanged and the job of moving the piano, the sculptures, and the pedestals was underway. Gus opened the big bay doors onto the loading dock, the cube van backed up and the hydraulic lift positioned. The piano was rolled out, into the cube van and padded and secured by straps. Andy's sculptures were loaded along with the pedestals and the three of them went back in to say goodbye to and thank Gus.

Ron told Gus that his recording had come out real good and thanked him some more for the help. "Any time, you guys. That was some good time."

Andy told Bill and Ron he was going to leave the piano in the van until tomorrow and said he would need their help then. He would take the van back to the house and asked Ron to stop on his way to HP if he had the time.

Ron was at Andy's before he got there and guided him in backing the van up to the garage. "Let's have a little talk if you have a few minutes." Andy requested and the two of them went inside. Ron knew what this was about, or at least he thought he did.

"The recording is so good you will pass out when you hear it." Ron was beaming with pride and handed Andy a CD. "Why don't you put that in your stereo."

Andy did and punched play on the changer for the

number one CD where he had placed it. Out came *Rhap-sody* so good it shocked Andy. He looked at Ron and saw the biggest smile he had ever seen on the guy. They just listened for a few minutes and it stayed good. Andy turned to Ron. "Recording studio?"

"Yes."

"First CD."

"Yes."

They shook hands and Andy asked Ron "Can Jan and I come over this evening and have a talk with you and Stefanie."

Ron replied. "We were already planning on that. We have a lot to talk about."

"Yes we do. Yes we do."

The two friends walked out to the street and Ron headed back to work and Andy went to the cube van. He slid open the over head door and climbed up into the box. He lifted the padding covering the Fallboard and Music Shelf and placed his hands on the Shelf and waited. It was gone. Nothing. He went around to the contour on the Case and placed his hand on the very place he had the first time he had touched the piano. Again there was nothing. Just the feel of cool, high gloss black lacquer on fine wood. Andy was ready for this and his only thought was that it was okay. He had his reward for saving this beautiful in-strument and it was time for someone who actual knew how, and was good enough, to play it as it should be played. Tomorrow it would be where it now belonged.

CHAPTER 51

Andy pulled into Ron and Stefanie's driveway and stopped, looking at Jan he asked her, "You are alright with this, aren't you?"

"Oh yes, Andy. We have already decided it is the right thing to do. We both know that."

They had discussed how to approach Ron and Stefanie about some kind of partnership that would benefit them both and also place the piano in good hands. Andy's assumption was that Ron wanted to get into the music production business. His sound studio build up was the obvious sign of his real interest. And Stefanie's stated desire to use her abilities as a concert level pianist were not being satisfied by teaching, even as much as she enjoyed it, at the high school.

Andy had told Jan that his contact with the piano was over. That there was no doubt about that and that he could no longer play at any level without whatever that magic was the piano had offered to him. It was over and they had to decide what to do with it. The garage was not an answer and to sell it wasn't either. Not that selling wasn't the logical course to take, as there was a lot of money involved, but Andy couldn't shake the idea that the piano was family.

As they walked up to the front door they could hear the familiar sound of a piano playing *Clair de lune* and when the door opened a familiar voice saying, "Sergei Rachmaninoff. It's your turn." Andy thought timing is everything as he and Jan were greeted by two very happy young people in their spectacular home.

They settled in comfortable chairs in that special room that Ron had built with glasses of wine, listening to the final part of Andy's playing Rachmaninoff's *Concerto No. 2,* while watching the sun slowly set behind the Colorado Rocky Mountains. Words weren't required yet and when the applause came over the speakers it was time for Andy to smile. Gus had been right, he had captured the house.

Ron touched a remote button and the system fell silent. He asked, "What are you thinking?" the question being directed to Andy.

Andy took in a breath. "A lot. . .And it is going to take some time to get to what is important. So here goes." He shifted his position so he was seated facing Ron and Stefanie. Jan slid her chair over to be right next to Andy.

"There is something you need to know about not only me but also about the piano. Stefanie will understand somewhat but you, poor Ron, will have to leave all rational thinking behind and accept what I am about to tell you as the truth."

Ron was not expecting this as Andy had just heard his fantastic recording of the concert already on a marketable CD and was thinking this was what the meeting was all about. Stefanie also was thinking along those lines but she immediately switched to the experience she had had when playing Andy's piano. Both sat still and waited.

Andrew's Piano

Andy leaned forward, elbows on knees with his hands out, fingers spread. "When I first touched that piano at the foundry auction I had a sensation I can only describe as touching something that was alive. I took my hand away and then touched it again. It was almost sensual, running through my hands, up my arms and into my chest. The sounds of the auction muted and the lights dimmed. It was surreal. I did it one more time and the effect was even stronger. That is why, without any thought, I bid on it."

Ron looked as if was having a hard time with this but Stefanie's look was as if a revelation had just occurred. Andy didn't pause. "Jan knows this story and I told Jason, who promised to keep it a secret which he has. When Stefanie played the piano that first time, and I am sure you remember that, I had the over whelming desire to learn how to play my piano. I had played with the Action, the keyboard, before it was even installed, pretending to be a pianist. Also, I found I could listen to music carefully and remember the notes. The night Stefanie played, after all of you had left, I tried to play the first few bars of *Rhapsody* and it worked. All I needed was to place my hands on the piano, sense that magic feeling and I was playing what I had memorized. I didn't have to think about anything but the music."

"You got to be kidding me," was Ron's response but Stefanie reached over and grabbed his arm. "No he's not Ron. That is exactly what happened to me. Exactly. I didn't have to think, just play the music. It was . . .magic."

They sat back and tried to recover. Each in deep thought, all on separate channels. All except Andy. "That magic for me is now gone. It left me immediately after the last key was struck on my encore. It is not there anymore. Not there last night or there this morning. It is over. I am okay with this. You may not understand why I am, but I am."

Andy then continued. "Now I want you two to listen carefully. Ron's CD of my concert is marketable. He can do others recordings, of you Stefanie playing the classics, and of you and Julia doing Broadway. Other pianist will want to record using a piano of this quality, and with Ron's ability to record their efforts it will draw them here. This is a unique opportunity for the two of you and Jan and I would like to be partners in this with you and we want my piano to be part of it."

Andy again paused. "I can't bring myself to sell it. My piano needs a new home. Yours."

Andrew's Piano

CHAPTER 52

The big party for Andrew's Piano in it's new home was planned by the ladies. It was one week after Andy and Jan's visit with Ron and Stefanie. At that visit, after some tears, confusion, hugs and happiness, the rough idea of a partnership was formed. In simple terms the piano would find it's new home in Ron's addition, would be part of a music recording partnership, and would become Stefanie's as Andy and Jan's returns on the partnership were realized. If for any reason the partnership was dissolved before that occurred, Stefanie and Ron would have first rights on the piano at the appraised value, modified by a formula that was agreed on. All income to Andy and Jan would be considered payment to them for their equity share of the piano.

Stevens Records came about with the first CD being "Andrew Miller Plays the Rialto." Ron had burned eighty, two disc sets, and made up a professional cover for the case, First Edition, each of which Andy laboriously signed. The first CD had the main concert from the light applause at the start to the rousing response at the finish. The second CD had the Encore recording with the call for more and applause at the finish. A total of 96 minutes.

As the team arrived the atmosphere was electric.

Art Myers

Eight people, covering almost three generations, all bound together by the beautiful Steinway Model C Parlor Grand Piano that now stood in the middle of a great room back dropped by the Colorado Rocky Mountain peaks. Julia, Stefanie and Ron the youngsters in their late twenties, Bill in his middle thirties, Jan and Andy in their early fifties, and Roberta and Jason, their late sixties. All good friends and for all intensive purposes a close family.

Some wine was drunk, some excellent food eaten, the music was Andy's concert recording, and later Stefanie played a few numbers and she and Julia did several popular show songs. Talk was on all subjects. The new partnership. Bill's big leap in sculpture with his new style. Ron's recording equipment including his 10.5 inch reel to reel that had just enough time on one reel to record all of Andy's main program.

Near the end of the evening each was provided ten first edition and signed "Andrew Miller Plays the Rialto" CDs with the advice to hang on to them as they will become collector's items.

As Andy and Jan drove home, Jan asked Andy if he would drive by Third and Jefferson, just a half block from his studio. He did as he was asked.

"Park right here," Jan told him as he was in front of the darkened three story building on the South-West corner of the intersection.

"Okay."

"Let's take a little walk around," Jan said as she opened the car door and got out. Andy did likewise and came over to her side. He had been seeing this building almost everyday for the last two years and often parked his van in the city parking lot to it's West side. It was somewhat run down, the yard a mess, a big asphalt parking lot on the South side, and seldom seemed occupied. It did have one of Loveland's biggest blue spruce trees on the lot's North-East corner.

"Yes?"

"I just got the listing for this place. Today in fact." Jan's voiced sounded a bit odd but Andy played along.

"And?" asked Andy, letting the question linger.

"You have to see it inside. It's a mess now but the bones are there. 1893. Fabulous woodwork. It could be renovated and make a beautiful home for us. The open attic is big, has great light and could be your studio. We could even do a bed & breakfast. I just sense something special about this place. That it is for us."

Andy smiled. "Let's take a closer look tomorrow."

Jan took Andy's hand thinking, "It would work out. It always did."

EPILOUGE

Twenty years later finds Andy's team all living, in good health, prosperous and happy. Could life be much better than this for them. A statement and not a question.

Ron and Stefanie's lives will make a dramatic change as Ron Stevens's Recording Studio ambition proved to be a very good move. The first product being "Andrew Miller Plays The Rialto" turned out to be wildly successful paving the way for several more CDs featuring "Stefanie Stevens Plays The Model C" and "Stefanie's & Julia's Broadway" also doing very well. Even today Ron's studio has as much business as he can handle. A separate building was built for most recording sessions but Andrew's Piano, now belonging to Stefanie and where it was meant to be, is used for all formal piano recordings. Stefanie is still the beloved music teacher at Loveland High School.

Jason and Roberta Roberts are approaching their 90's in good health and happiness. Jason plays the Steinway in their living room every morning for half an hour as Roberta fixes breakfast. A second half hour before dinner each night, and any time friends come over for socializing. He is, and knows he is, playing his vintage Steinway better than ever. They both were involved in the early setup of Ron Stevens's recording studio business with Roberta doing legal and book keeping and Jason advising on studio management.

Bill and Julia are still in love and in love with life.

Their twin boys are juniors in high school, remarkably good looking, smarter than anyone deserves to be, immensely popular and single digit handicap golfers. Julia's success with Stefanie has not only brought financial rewards but even a number of professional performance opportunities. Bill's sculpture continues, to this day, to be popular and rewards him accordingly. With some good intended ribbing by Andy and Jan, Bill and Julia got married on their twin's fourth birthday. The ceremony was held next to a beautiful Steinway Parlor Grand Piano with the Colorado Rocky Mountains in the background.

Andy and Jan bought the house on the Third Street and Jefferson Ave corner. It took Andy, with some help from Jan, six months to renovate and it became their beautiful home, the Andy Miller Studio and the Jefferson House Bed & Breakfast. Andy's sculpture career continued until five years ago when his last life size commissioned piece was installed in Illinois. Jan was successful in real estate sales and suggested to Andy, about this time, that a change of course might be in order. The B & B was closed and shortly there after the house was sold to a young family of five. A year and a half of car travel, various rentals and stays with friends was followed by them buying a 42 foot sailboat in Newport Beach, California. Neither had ever been on a boat before, but they are currently somewhere on the water in the Pacific Northwest.

Just last week, on a particular fine fall Saturday afternoon a recently divorced young mother and her son were riding their bicycles along the road that fronted the Stevens's home. The boy, age ten, was out ahead as they headed up the gentle incline and he stopped at the top near the Stevens's drive way. He heard some music coming from the house and was immediately taken by it's sound and tone. His last few years had been very unpleasant for him with his parent's separation and his feeling of being deserted by his father. His mother was trying her best but with her full time job and problems with child support had left the two of them in an very difficult situation.

When his mother stopped next to him and started to speak, the young boy said, "Shush, listen to that." She did and was also taken by what she was hearing. Just then Ron started down the driveway to check for the mail. He knew immediately what was happening as Stefanie had opened the side windows and was busy playing her piano. She was at that moment playing *Rhapsody In Blue* and even to his ear was giving it a special meaning. Ron walked up to the young boy and said, "That is something very special, don't you think?"

"Oh yes, sir. What is it? Who's doing it? It's wonderful."

Ron looked at the boy's mother and smiled. She smiled back with a somewhat embarrassed and surprised look. "It is wonderful. Is that a recording?"

"No, that's my wife playing one of her favorites. Would you like to come up to the house and listen inside? She loves to play for an audience and the sound is even better indoors."

The young mother hesitated, but when she saw the pleading look in her son's eyes she said, "That would be so nice. So nice of you."

"My name is Ron Stevens and what is your name, young man?"

"My name is Andrew Moore, but everybody calls me Andy."

ABOUT THE AUTHOR

Art Myers was born in 1935 and grew up in the small southern California town of La Mesa. He graduated from San Diego State College in 1958 with a BS Degree in Engineering. Several employments in the Military Industrial Complex lasted until end of 1969. His first layoff was in 1961 and he spent the fall months working as construction labor in Mammoth Lakes, CA and the winter of 1962 skiing in Aspen, Colorado. Another stint in engineering and a second layoff occurred which found him with a wife, daughter, house payments and just beginning what became a 30 year career as a professional sculptor. Interspersed in that 30 years were a variety of residences and occupations for both he and his wife. Retiring in 2002 they bought a sail boat and spent 10 years living aboard and cruising both US coasts. They have lived in a variety of places including Saratoga, CA, Aspen and Loveland, CO, Lake Forest, IL and currently in Vero Beach, FL.

His first book was an autobiography written for family and friends in 2015. ANDREW'S PIANO is his first work of fiction.

www.ingramcontent.com/pod-product-compliance
Lightning Source LLC
Chambersburg PA
CBHW070531100726
47907CB00004B/1075